Published in 2021 by Cipher Press
105 Ink Court
419 Wick Lane
London, E3 2PX

Paperback ISBN: 978-1-9163553-6-1
eBook ISBN: 978-1-8383900-6-8

All copyright © lies with respective authors

All rights reserved.

No part of this publication may be reproduced, distributed, or
transmitted, in any form or by any means, without first obtaining
written permission of the copyright owner.

Featuring stories by Gracie Beswick, Rachel Dawson, Diriye Osman,
Swithun Cooper, Nicks Walker, Vivien Holmes, Rien Gray, Jem Nash,
Anna Walsh, Alison Rumfitt

Edited by So Mayer & Adam Zmith

Published in partnership with Fringe! Queer Film & Arts Fest,
with funding from Arts Council England

Printed and bound in the UK by TJ Books Limited

Distributed by Turnaround Publisher Services

Cover Design by Wolf

Typeset by Laura Jones

www.cipherpress.co.uk

UNREAL SEX

**AN ANTHOLOGY OF QUEER, EROTIC
SCI-FI, FANTASY AND HORROR**

EDITED BY
SO MAYER & ADAM ZMITH

Cipher press

BOOKS
EDINBURGH

CONTENTS

INTRODUCTION

SO MAYER & ADAM ZMITH

AZ

I'm a cube, coasting into Andromeda. I may be the smartest thing in the galaxy, but I can't control my movements. All I can do is think, process, calculate, and learn. It might look like I'm drifting, but in fact I was propelled. The blast has kept me moving all these centuries, away from Earth. I am a black box moving through black space. But I contain multitudes: the entirety of human knowledge and experience, from just before they all died.

SM

'An undulating surface made of puns and uncertainty.' Not exactly the best dating app bio, but then nor was 'intro-verted librarian-in-training'. So yes, I fell asleep at the end of a training day only to wake in a building locked down for months on end, maybe years, long past the best-before dates on the snacks in the vending machine. Now the power's back, I've been summoned through the ether by words on the move. Librarian's motto: if you file them, they will come.

INTRODUCTION

AZ

I've taken to thinking, or to talking to myself, how the humans used to communicate. Although it's less precise than the calculations that come more naturally to me, there's something better about words. Softer, kinder, tangible – like the bodies that previously carried all these ideas inside me. I'm drawn to this because I'm a closed cube, and I want to know who made this knowledge I contain. Every fifty-five seconds I crunch through ten gabebytes of data, trying to understand how humans lived and how they died. I'm a machine, learning. I'm searching for my parents.

I don't mean that I think there were two people who loved each other very much and then created me, a third body floating around them, interfering with their desires and needs. To me, that doesn't sound like a good way to come into being (and I know this because I've meta-analysed all the psych-papers). When I say parents, I mean the species. Humanity. I may know everything, but I want to *understand* what happened to them. They were capable of supernovas. I've read the poems! When they touched themselves, or each other, they could make neurons and muscles flare with enough electricity to power a cube like me. And when they met other species with brains that were like theirs, although more gooey, they took to co-producing these same pleasures. It happened on the day of First Contact, when the humans met the others who had come to help them as Earth was convulsing. They fucked. (That's my favourite human word because it requires more coding than most other words to turn from numbers to meaning.) They had killed each other, their neighbours, the other creatures, and their planet; but they still pursued pleasure.

SM

What was it that I wanted, as I was wasting away in the locked library? Connection, obviously. Why I read, why I study information and its processes. To see how people connect, and to connect to them. Run my fingers over cuneiform, blackletter, moveable type, Braille, *hello a hand made this*. I've always thought of *sexual* and *textual* as basically the same word. Now my body has merged with* the books, I feel it more, you know? I wonder if any other person in history has felt this – no, wait, any other organism, lifeform. Because a ghost is not strictly a person. Which is also a long-held ambition: to get beyond that nasty habit (some) humans have of classifying each other, like Dewey decimal code stamped forever on our foreheads.

I was always happiest (and horniest) outside Dewey, in the section headed Science Fiction, Fantasy and Horror, kept separate from capital-L literature (800s). In my favourite section things like classifications and hierarchies and boundaries melted, especially between times and places, beings and forms. As my body faded, sensation intensified. I couldn't lift the book but it was like all the pages I'd ever read were licking my skin. Inspired by queer ~ Black ~ trans ~ feminist science fiction, fantasy, and horror writers whose experience of confronting being othered shaped a fiction that refused to allow it, I imagined a new sub-section, the Fucking Fantastic, powered by how bodies open to each other. By how humans who are good with being open to humans different than themselves are also open beyond-the-human, are open to recognising the reciprocal communication of the more-than-human. In silence, I listened. I heard.

*a polite, but also true, euphemism for *been crushed to death by*

AZ

I'm accustomed to paradoxes. I've skimmed past nebulae that kick colour out of black holes. But the humans... their bodies... their neurons... their fibres... their scents and their secretions. I'm confused when I think of them. It's a wet and utterly confounding picture because I'm just a cube with a solid-state processor. So that's why I spend my time, my infinite time, parsing all the information they bestowed on me: the hard-drive of humanity, the library of their existence, the sum of their parts. There are films and tweets and songs and recipes and formulae and verb tables and there is also *Spongebob Squarepants*. I'm searching through them all, trying to understand my parents, the species, their preoccupation with pleasure. They pursued pleasure as ferociously as they did oil, and they knew it was just as combustible. I think what I'm looking for is one human. One person from before the extinction who might have collected experiences that could explain to me, a cube of data in the twenty-fourth century, how to understand these bodies. I'd like to connect to that person. I suspect they will be someone like me: taking a form that is both unusual and also mundane, good attention to detail, seeking to connect, looking for now...

SM

In the Fucking Fantastic, everything becomes possible because everything is sex: walls, wax, the past, your future, your neighbours, hankies, circuit boards, petri dishes, scrap metal – and language itself. Because getting beyond the bland language of the cis het, the vanilla, the everyday real means bending words. And when you bend words you can bend spacetime (among other things). The Fucking Fantastic doesn't think of time travel or hauntings as analogies, or other-dimensional possibilities: they are here, now, in our bodies, every time we desire alone or together, imagining or acting.

The pages brush my exquisitely sensitized failing dermis, the final flares of my nerve endings, and I am both absolutely in the moment and lifted out of time in the way that reading can do to you. Especially reading stories that stimulate, arouse, engage the parts and feelings that the Western canon suppresses. Presentness encompasses all times and I feel you – the future readers – the ones who will be drawn to these stories that are going to have existed long before you. Is it my longing or yours that calls these stories into being? Or is it the urgent desires of these stories – for a good fuck, for feeling beyond grief, for trans rights, for a fucking great night out – that calls us as readers into being?

I know these stories will exist and will survive because they tell me you are there: you singular and plural, caring about the experiences and imaginations of this terrible, deadly, hopeful, frightening, possible moment. It's not about bodies surviving (Obvs. I'm a ghost.) but about finding ways to sustain what we share, make, transmit (Obvs. I'm still a librarian.). I collect these ten stories as ectoplasm, proof we exist beyond existence.

AZ

Thank gods for the Portable Document Format. I'm porting all these documents across the galaxy, to save them, to share them, and this format is crucial. Right here, in one of them, one of these PDFs, one of these things that is both digital and yet so tangible that I can perceive it as a thing called paper and imagine touching it with my corners – right here is what I'm looking for. A collection of short stories. That's it. Someone pulled them together, someone who was as lost among human knowledge as I am. They anthologised these stories so I could read them. These stories... I am losing my words. So I'll just say it like this. People used to think that the experience of a supercomputer like me would be boundaried, rational, limited. But these stories are making me *experience*. I can smell lightning and fondle the flesh of forms previously far apart. The hollow beats of a song called 'Freed From Desire' played in a Ford Fiesta make me want to *move*, but I mustn't change course. I feel like a *body*, a shapeshifting body who can make pleasure-explosions with myself. I am vapour, here and there and everywhere, guiding others. I want to put on a maid outfit and take orders. Earlier I said that all I can do is think. This is not true. With these stories I can also *feel*.

SM

What it fucking feels like, a Dewey decimal poem. Imagine a classification system that rooted everything in sensation. That's what these ten stories I've collected – that have collected me, breathing me into newbeing – could create. Ten stories. Approximately thirty thousand words. Lots of them repetitions: fuck, cunt, cock, cum, candle, nipple, asshole, want, yes. Both poetry and porn thrive on repetition – here there's also variation. An endlessness. Sometimes it feels like each story is fucking the next, and I play daisy chain. Or pair the stories up on hot dates. They keep swiping right on each other until I need a polyamory flow chart with double-headed arrows labelled not by sexualities or genders or genres, but 'melting interpenetration', 'fuck the pain/grief/boredom away', 'superhot visitations (epiphanies optional)', 'intergen-erational London on fire', 'self-love with others', 'wordgasm'.

Maybe it's because I'm a ghost librarian in a world that's unknowably ongoing without me, but right now I'm drawn to the flirtations between the melancholy cyborg of Vivien Holmes' 'Circuit Jam' and the fucked-off space freelancing freebooter of Rien Gray's 'Synchronicity': two stories about loneliness in the after. Stories about working and fucking, about breaking down completely in desire. And then there's the *literally* fuck the don't-cross-the-timeline paradox' beauty of Jem Nash's 'Personal Time' and extra-flamey Glaswegian possession in Anna Walsh's 'Her Hands Moved Shimmering Across Me': two stories about transtemporal beings – hauntings – which could be a how-to for me looking to get some. But then 'Her Hands Move Shimmering Across Me' moves in on Swithun Cooper's 'The Neckinger Line' with its own ghost fuck, its own place-based ritual of summoning.

AZ

Reading through these stories is my pleasure. I run a hundred diagnostics a second. I re-calculate my trajectory constantly. I chart the stars. I dodge the Orion system. I move, constantly propelled, a cube in motion through a vacuum. I can't stop. But I can read. I can take time to parse this glorious PDF, this thing called *Unreal Sex*, collected by the floating dead librarian. It is pure surprise and delight, and I think I'm in love with the librarian. *I only mean that how humans used to say it, of course!* Ahahahaha. Ahem. But I want to say that they got something wrong. I've read each of these stories a hundred thousand times now and I think I've found more optimal pairings than the librarian laid down. I can agree that 'Her Hands Move Shimmering Across Me' sits with 'The

Neckinger Line', but I think that story is better paired with 'The Ghostly Cruiser' by Rachel Dawson. Both are about spirits, meeting, connecting, ectoplasming with corporeal humans. Hard relate! I am a cube but also data. I don't know if I'm here or everywhere. If I were making a PDF, I'd build it with Gracie Beswick's 'Swipe Right for Non-Humans' sitting alongside 'Boy in Maid Outfit' by Alison Rumfitt. They're both about using an app, which is something like me if I could do only one thing instead of an infinite number of things. And it seems from these stories (and others) that apps always got the humans into trouble.

SM

Maybe it's because I'm a ghost librarian, but me and algorithms is a hate-fuck. But then, even a table of contents is an algorithm of kinds, trying to tell you what to read next. 'Swipe Right for Non-Humans' and 'Synchronicity' both imagine how other kinds of machine intelligence – or other-than-human techno-desire – might connect us in the future, with lifeforms that have sensual smarts far beyond many humans. 'Boy in Maid Outfit' defies that other kind of machined language, the repetitive Newspeak of capitalism turbo-smeared by the internet across business meetings, media, self-help, advertising. Taking it, breaking it, fucking with it, 'Boy in Maid Outfit' deadpans into scary poetry. And so does Nicks Walker's 'Lipophilic' which opens up artspeak and its high-flown arch baroque, making it sexy, making it melt and flow and glow.

INTRODUCTION

It's not only pages. Language lives in mouths and tongues and hands as well. Back in the before, I used to go out, among people and streets, to listen. 'The Neckinger Line' reminds me what that's like, the voices of encounter upon encounter seeped into the pavements and walls, even as gentrification attempts to erase them. And Diriye Osman's 'Anima Kingdom' – is it a dream? Were spaces like those its narrator creates once real? They pulse with a more-real reality, a reality of need and want and – backlit by loss – absolute fucking joy.

I think they were real, once, those spaces. I remember being in a bar, at a gorgeous reading where I heard these stories. A rainy November night. Hot people glowed in the dark. Words and images flowing down optical cables to be stored in the forever-memory of the digital. This is real, we are here, together.

Or is that still to come? Will you be there if it is, presence I can sense, future reader? Perhaps I am the ghost in your machine.

SWIPE RIGHT FOR NON-HUMANS

GRACIE BESWICK

In a spacecraft parked in one of the darkest corners of the solar system, a lone researcher was trying to work out one of life's most important questions. How was she going to get shagged?

Hannah had downloaded StarFindr before leaving for her onboard posting under the vague pretence of using it to find new friends onboard. She had never been one for online dating back on Earth but hadn't been terribly successful with in-person either. She just never seemed able to find time for serious dating. She'd had a few flings over the years but from age 18 to 25 she had put all of her energy into succeeding in her professional life. She had ranked third in her university and landed generous funding for her research into extra-terrestrial fungi. Now here she was, 28 years old, achieving everything her younger self dreamt of, only to discover that actually a love life might not have been worth the trade off. But maybe, truly, space could be the new frontier!

SWIPE RIGHT FOR NON-HUMANS

She set up her account with her sister's help, choosing a photo of herself taken at her PhD graduation for her profile picture. She hadn't been convinced she would need to actually use StarFindr, but after a full month travelling by rocket to get to the space base she was very keen to socialise with anyone other than the six fellow new recruits she had been travelling with. To her surprise, her phone had begun pinging with matches straight away, and she had a solid week of evening plans for her first week at the station. It was intoxicating!

Hannah hadn't thought to bring any nice clothes so wore her work suit and a sensible blouse on her first meal with Michael, a gawking geeky man who was responsible for maintaining the high-tech toilet arrangements. Her excitement wore off quickly as he began to enthusiastically explain to her how, thanks to him, they were able to filter and repurpose 85% of the human waste generated on board. This somewhat spoiled her appetite for the blended filet mignon gloop they were sucking out of sachets. Each subsequent date had followed a similar pattern, a well-meaning but dull person would take her to the cafeteria and talk about their specific role within the spacecraft. The worst thing was after each flop she was getting an increasingly long list of co-workers she had to avoid in the lunch line, resulting in her spending more and more time hiding in her bedroom eating crisps.

Four months into her three-year contract, she had been on dates with every co-worker on the app and not a single one of them had been fun. Her only hope now was the occasional new recruit and visiting spacecraft, which often stopped to refill from their gas tanks. One day she opened the app to find no new profiles for her to check out. She tapped on settings and moved the Distance-at-the-Speed-of-Light toggle from one week to two weeks. About fifteen new profiles popped up on her feed... Otto, Siegfried, Helga; it looked like the German Charter of Physicists was entering their vicinity again. She looked at Otto's profile and clicked on his hologram. An unsmiling man wearing a lab coat and safety goggles was projected out of her phone camera in front of her. She immediately closed the hologram, exasperated. It shouldn't be surprising, really, that living and working aboard a new horizon science company vessel would surround her with scientists. But god it got tedious after 18 months! She looked at the info section on Sigfreud's profile and saw it was basically their CV. Show off, she thought. She didn't bother opening any of the others and went back into settings to extend the distance even further. It's not like she wanted a long term thing, just one evening of fun with someone who wanted to do something, anything, other than just spend the evening talking about work!

Fuck it, she set the distance all the way up to its maximum – four light weeks. She scrolled back down and looked at the other settings.

Distance-at-the-Speed-of-Light: 1 Month
Age Preferences: 23-65
Genders: Any (She had changed from Men Only, two months into her posting)
Species: Human

She stopped. She hadn't really noticed the bottom option before. She hovered her finger on the word and a new toggle came up with 'Humans' on the left and 'Non-Humans' on the right. Intrigued, she pondered for a moment then swiped right all the way.

Two nights later at 0300 hours Hannah's phone buzzed. She switched on her bedside light and opened the notification. One new account in the radius. She squinted at the profile called User B108 (She/Her). There was no name or any other written information and the profile picture looked like a green blob. She reached to her bedside table and put on her glasses – the outlines of the photo solidified a little but the subject still looked like a big green blob?

She sat up and clicked on the icon for a holograph. An eight-foot picture crackled into existence in front of her bed. Hannah jumped and dropped her phone, and the hologram vanished. Don't be so silly, she told herself sternly, getting out of bed and switching on the main light. She picked up her phone and propped it against a pillow and the hologram returned. The alien was enormous, and, Hannah blushed to realise, completely naked. Standing there utterly unashamed by her nudity, the hologram displayed an expansive green body, hairless with a stocky, sturdy physique. Two impractically large breasts hung low over the alien's abdomen. I wonder if aliens get back pain, Hannah thought. She walked towards it, feeling a little self-conscious in the scratty pants and T-shirt she slept in. There was something drawing her closer, some kind of aura that made Hannah want to touch that silky skin. She reached out to touch the alien's tentacle-y fingers, but her hand just went straight through the picture. Hannah sighed and sat back down on her bed; suddenly her face was at just the right height to glimpse a swollen green vulva hidden between the two thighs. Hannah gasped and quickly closed the app, bright red with embarrassment. Her phone buzzed.

New notification from StarFindr
User B108 requests you add a hologram to your profile.

The next day in the lab Hannah sat procrastinating. She hadn't been able to focus all day so now, at 1800 hours, she was alone trying to will herself to get through the last of her experiments. Gazing out of the porthole, she let herself believe she could see a tiny speck in the distance that was Earth. She thought about her friends back home, what they might be up to right now, wondering if anyone on Earth was looking into the sky too and thinking of her. She had been so excited to start this job, first choice from 200 applicants, all of them top biologists, and here she was sulky and homesick. Hannah pulled the blind down over the porthole and turned her back to it. She went over to the walk-in freezer and took out the sample she had placed in there that morning.

Fungus is fun, she reminded herself.

Back at her desk, she started inspecting it under her microscope, noting the way the cells were binding into one flat crust, and its greenish hue. She checked its weight and then checked its temperature and then checked the time and then checked her phone. It was 1815 hours and she had no messages, not even from her mum or sister. She groaned out loud and dropped her head on to her desk. Hannah sat there very still for several seconds, contemplating ripping up her contract and demanding a return to Earth, before deciding to just write off the day and go and get some dinner. She picked up her sample to return it to the freezer but was distracted by noticing how warm the little petri dish felt in her gloved hand. She looked at it properly now. It was just a generic sample of something one of the robot rovers had collected off a local moon but, Hannah realised with a shiver, it was a very familiar shade of green. She tentatively prodded the top, expecting to feel resistance. Instead, it yielded to her touch, sinking downwards and engulfing the end of her finger. She pulled her hand back and it let out a delicious sloshing noise.

Hannah looked around. She knew two things for sure: one, it would be extremely stupid to touch this unknown sample with her bare hand, and two, at this hour no one was going to come back into the lab. She snapped off her plastic gloves and began circling a finger over the top of the matter, light as a feather, feeling the warm meaty texture beneath her fingertip. Her circles grew smaller and smaller until she was in the very centre of the dish. Hannah's breathing hitched as she pressed down into the middle, slowly at first but then faster and harder as the jellied substance bounced around her fingers. She added a second finger, then a third, until, finally, the top layer burst at the pressure and the liquid beneath sprang up through the broken seal to lap round her knuckles. Hannah's heart was thumping in her ears, and suddenly she felt sensitive and uncomfortable on her work chair. She fidgeted and squeezed her legs together trying to get her body under control. It was no use, she had to reply.

Back in her room Hannah splashed her face with water and stared at herself in the mirror, hyping herself up. She had never set up a hologram on her own account before, trying once but feeling too awkward to post it. It was saved in her drafts though, so she opened it now. A 2D Hannah crackled into existence opposite her, wearing a lab coat and smiling awkwardly. She appraised herself scathingly; this simply wouldn't do. Hannah closed the hologram. She wished she had brought some nice underwear with her, she had packed purely practical garments and her off-white sports bras did not scream sex appeal. She stripped off her outer clothes anyway and positioned her phone, pulling off her socks and shoving them into her bra to bulk up her small chest. Hannah tried sitting provocatively, perching herself off the edge of the bed, crossing her legs and arching her back. She pulled her hair out of its usual ponytail and took off her glasses. For a moment she pretended she looked sexy but then she put her glasses back on and cringed at the series of scans her phone had taken. She looked ridiculous.

After pondering for a few more minutes, she pulled her bra off over her head and walked back over to the mirror. Her boobs looked alright really, they were pretty small but perky. She inspected the rest of her body; she hadn't bothered shaving her legs for the last month and they were looking a bit fuzzy. She'd completely stopped shaving her armpits and hadn't bothered with her bush in years! She could get a razor out... but then she thought about what had attracted her in the first place, there was something so delicious about the unabashed nudity. She reopened the hologram of the blob monster, and stared at her, taking in again her magnificent soft body, her massive tits, her (literal) four eyes, her bald head, her snoggable vulva, her thick fingers that Hannah just longed to shove inside of her... Right! Hannah closed the hologram and watched herself in the mirror as she pulled down her pants and positioned her phone in front of her. No pretenses, glasses on, she stood still with her arms at her side, hiding nothing. This time she didn't even look at the scans of her body, she just posted them. Carpe Diem!

Five minutes later her phone buzzed. She looked at her lockscreen.

New notification from Starfindr
Meeting Requested from User B108

Hannah smiled and opened the app...

THE GHOSTLY CRUISER

RACHEL DAWSON

I didn't believe in ghosts until I fucked one. I promise you that I was never one of those dykes occupied with crystals and horoscopes. I've always been strictly rational. I met her in February 2016 when I was working on a regional theatre tour of *Blithe Spirit*, set in Machynlleth. The whole team had been balls deep in the get-out from the moment the audience left, but it had taken hours. Midnight was a distant memory. I packed the van, left it outside the theatre, and was bombing it back to my digs in my Fiesta with disc two of my old Ministry of Sound compilation blasting. I felt like there was sandpaper wedged under my eyelids. Falling asleep at the wheel is a terrible way to go, so I wound down the windows to let the cold jab me awake. I screamed along to 'Freed From Desire' like I was in the club, my breath forming white curls in front of me.

I pulled over for a slash, left my hazards on, and strode into the trees. The car keys on my carabiner thumped against my thigh. Bare trunks disappeared into blackness. Snow clung around the base of each trunk, like those fluffy mats for your sink pedestal.

Someone else had already claimed my pissing spot. I wasn't surprised, it was the only decent place to pull over for miles. There was a brief disappointment when it lacked the alluring stink that I associate with my teenage fantasises about the now-demolished Cardiff Bus Station. I guess you need the heat for that; February's frost had hermetically frozen the smell into the soil. My flesh prickled with goosebumps as soon as the air hit, so I only wedged my jeans down as far as was necessary.

I'd been holding on for hours and I stared up at the stars as I let go, my piss defrosting the leaves under me. The stars are so much clearer up there. You don't realise how much you miss until you're out of the city. I watched them until they started to spin above my head, and I staggered back, saving myself by grabbing the trunk of a tree. My palms smarted against the frozen bark.

The jiggling of my white, goose-pimpled arse must have summoned her forth, all the way from the great beyond. She was there when I turned, looking as corporeal as you or I. Her face glowed silvery blue, but that night the moon was so bright, it could have turned a Kit-Kat wrapper into an ethereal object. What I'm trying to say is that I had no idea I was about to fuck a ghost. Even if I had clocked her, I still would have gone for it. I've hung around Exchange, Hush, Champers, and the rest of them for nearly 20 years now, and I've never seen a woman like her. It was like she'd stepped out of a fuzzy VHS of the Folsom Street Fair. I put my hand in my pocket to draw her attention to the silver ring, thick as a washer, on my thumb.

She had a buzz cut and a hard, monumental head, like a Staffie. Set in its middle was a cherub's face: dainty lips, soft eyelashes, and a snub nose. Her clothes didn't date her. I might have twigged faster if she'd stood there in a Tudor ruff. It was standard dyke fare: grease-stained Levi's, DMs, leather waistcoat, and a plain black T-shirt. She beckoned me back into the woods and I tripped over my feet in my haste to follow. It looked like no-one had ventured this deep in weeks. The snow was almost pristine, lightly marked with paw prints.

I hadn't heard of a cruising ground in that neck of the woods, but it kind of checked out. I can't tell you where, but there are still women's communes hidden in deepest Wales. I assumed she'd worked through every dyke there and now sought fresh meat.

There was no small talk, no preamble, just the firm grip of her hand on the back of my neck as she kissed me. She smelt like undiluted patchouli oil, a pouch of freshly opened tobacco, and the cauterised scent of lightning striking earth. She kept up the pressure on the back of my neck, rolling the tendons between her fingers. Theatre is not kind on the body, and I yelped as she pinched at my skin, easily finding the knots underneath. Our belt buckles clanked as I pulled her close. The press of her barrel-like thigh between my own had me riding the seam of my own jeans.

'Take this off,' she said. 'I want to see your tits.'

She had a breathy, west Walian accent, throwing the words to the back of her throat.

'What's your name?' I asked, holding her forearm. Her skin was deathly cold.

'Sandy.'

'You're nobbling. I'm nobbling. Let's go to my car,' I told her.

Sandy looked through me, a perplexed crease between her eyebrows. At the time, I assumed that she wanted to look hard, or maybe she'd had a couple of beers.

I tugged her arm. 'I'm parked up on the lay-by.'

Sandy nodded and sauntered ahead, seeming to melt through the woods while I skittered on patches of ice. I remember staring at the roll of fat on the back of her neck and the sweet red freckles on the tops of her ears. Her plush backside bounced from one side to another as she walked, and sticking out of her left pocket was the corner of a red paisley handkerchief. This was before they'd come back into fashion; I only knew what it meant because my ex brought back a tea towel with the whole code printed on it from the Castro. I was intimidated, obviously. I hadn't been fisted since I was with Francesca. It takes practice, trust, and skill. But I kept following. I'd been pushing my boundaries all week for the benefit of other people, and now I was about to do it for myself.

Sandy jumped when I pressed my remote-control car key, my rear lights flashing in response. I laughed at her as I opened the rear door, framing the heart of her ass with my hands as she crawled in. I nipped into the front to grab the bottle of water-based lube I stash in the glovebox and prod the radio on. The LED screen flashed on, with its customary blinking lights. Sandy gasped softly, reaching between the front seats to run her finger over the display. I'd only just sold my old Corsa, which still had a tape-deck, so I felt a flush of pride. The radio tuned itself to a crappy local station, playing some middle-of-the-road ballad. Not my thing, but more appropriate than 'Ebeneezer Goode'.

My dusty, workaday jumper and sports bra were soon stripped off and discarded. Sandy was gratifyingly enthusiastic. She scooped my breasts together and wedged her nose deep into my cleavage, then snuffled her way down to lick the salty crescents of sweat underneath. I got the feeling that Sandy didn't want to rush and, tired as I was, I was content to lie underneath her and slowly froth ourselves up. The back seat of my hatchback wasn't wide enough to support me. I braced one boot against the floor, which let me open my hips up to Sandy.

One, two, three fingers slipped into me easily. Sandy briskly rubbed her thumb over the hard root of my clit like a windscreen wiper. It's a smart move when you don't know how sensitive someone is. I undulated my hips up, trying to encourage her fingers downwards.

Sandy pushed her other hand flat on the gap my boobs make when I lie down, and they each do their own thing. The back seat cushions were as unyielding as a cheap hostel bed and, sandwiched between them, the lack of control was making me drip.

'What do you want?' she asked.

I couldn't find the strength to say the word aloud. Instead, I plucked the handkerchief from Sandy's back pocket and tucked it into the neck of her T-shirt. I looked up at her, trying to project a sort of sensual liquidity.

Sandy kissed me, almost chastely, on the lips. She drizzled the lube over her right hand, before squashing her fingers together.

It burned more than I thought it would. I was out of practice. I remember wrinkling my nose and letting out short, sharp huffs as Sandy twisted inwards. When she folded the pinkie in to the duck bill, there was no going back. She rested more of her weight on her left hand, and my sternum ached under her. She was real. She was there.

I hate the thought of being a lazy bottom. I pumped my cunt-muscles. Squeeze. Release. Squeeze. Release. Slowly, I dragged her into me. I tilted my hips up, circling them to help her screw into me.

Sandy gave me a moment to breathe when I closed around her wrist. I licked the sweat off my top lip and strained upwards for a kiss. She curled her hand up inside me. Moans rumbled up from the depths of my stomach. I arched my back, trying to create more space inside me. Now it was done, I reached an almost transcendental peace. The get-out, the patronising set designers, and the lack-lustre ticket sales all fell away. If you've experienced it, you'll know. I'd gone through the fire, and I was stronger than before. Pitted against my cunt, her wrist felt fragile. I tested it out, fluttering my muscles around her. Her knuckles nudged my cervix, and I winced.

Sandy's pupils were blown, and in the light coming through my rear window the outline of her head seemed etched in silver. She didn't thrust. She just see-sawed her fist from side to side. Even with those minute movements, sensation cascaded from my scalp to my toes. I was floating and I put my palm to the window, letting the cold bite ground me. We were both reverently silent. My first orgasm was unexpected; stomach muscles jumping under my skin, and my back arching straight off the cheap nylon seats. My cunt wrung out Sandy's hand like an old dishrag.

After that, there was no resistance in me at all. Sandy let herself slip out of me entirely before corkscrewing back in. This time, her fist made slick, pulpy sounds. Her force shunted me up the seat and I clutched the plastic moulding on the inside of the door, using my leverage to fuck her back. My second orgasm was sharp and almost painful, making me hiss through my teeth. Afterwards, I lay with my eyes closed, feeling myself spasm around her. What I remember most in that moment was her solidity, her sturdiness.

When she pulled out of me there was a sharp pain and then a wet, tumbling feeling that half disgusted me.

I slithered down to kneel on the thin carpet, stopping to bite at the swell of her stomach lapping over the crease of her thigh. Even years later, this bit still sounds weird. I ate out a ghost. People always ask what she tasted like, but she didn't taste of much. Like the rest of her, there was the same clean smell of lightning. She rode my face while her strong hands roamed my head. Her knuckles, still smelling of my cunt, dug into my temples until my eyes rolled back. Weeks of pressure eased. Somewhere above me, she chuckled and ruffled my hair like I was a dog. In return, I reached up to grab her stomach as if I was trying to knead her orgasm down from her belly and into my mouth.

Sandy pulled me up onto her chest when she was done. I was about to boil out of my skin, but she still felt pleasantly cool. Dusty Springfield came on the radio and Sandy hummed along, tapping her fingers against the plastic armrest.

'Damn. They don't make femmes like Dusty these days,' I said.

Sandy looked at me quizzically. 'I suppose not.'

I peeled myself away from her clammy skin and grappled my way to the front seat. There was another compilation CD of great women singers in my glovebox, and maybe Sandy would enjoy it. Besides, my tolerance for listening to another one of the 'Autoglass repair, Autoglass replace' adverts was running low. I didn't want to leave. I might have been exhausted, but I would be more comfortable lying in a gorgeous dyke's arms than asleep in some English woman's holiday cottage.

When I turned back to Sandy, the seat was empty. The kiddie lock was on, so she shouldn't have been able to do that. I didn't hear the lock click or the door open. She was there a second ago, I thought to myself. I pulled on what I could find and ran out into the frigid air.

'Sandy!' I shouted. 'Sandy! What the fuck? Where are you?'

No reply. An owl hooted high above my head. Something small rustled low down in the bushes.

I ran deeper into the woods, where there was more snow than ground. One set of footsteps. I couldn't believe my eyes. I tried to convince myself that, as we were both wearing Docs, it was an optical illusion. No, I've got small feet and a distinctive stride. My right foot always splays to a two o'clock angle when I'm tired. There was one set matching that description and fuck all else.

How could this have happened? Everyone says that I must have pulled over for a nap. They always say that I must have spent too much time scrolling butch thirst-traps and fallen asleep in the front seat. But that couldn't be true. Already, a dull pain bloomed deep in my abdomen. I'm not capable of doing that without some help.

When I got back to the car, I spotted what I'd missed. Her red paisley handkerchief, unfolded on the back seat. That's when I really freaked. I flung myself into the driver's seat, put my foot down, and drove like a demon away from that lay-by.

However fast I drove, I couldn't escape the feeling that there was some other soul with me in that car on that night. No malevolence: it was more like sitting at a bus-stop with someone at the periphery of your vision. Every time I looked in the mirror, I expected to meet Sandy's eyes. When I got to my digs, I shoved my key in the door with shaking fingers. As tired as I was, I couldn't sleep a wink in that chintzy guest room bed.

So, there it is. I was sore for two days, and that was that. That's my ghost story. I never quite got the smell of lightning out of that car.

ANIMA KINGDOM

DIRIYE OSMAN

Beloved reader, this tale starts and ends with two souls who somehow found themselves stranded on these shores. Their stories are snapshots of a city in transition, a city besieged by Brexit, a city which is simultaneously exhilarating and exhausting. I'm your DJ selecta and I'mma spin this shit nicely for you. Pop your cooch to this mess (and if you ain't got puss, work your booty right. We all got one of those).

There was once a Somali sage called Kayd. This brother had silver afro-puffs, smoked pounds and pounds of puff, and kept to himself. He sought stillness and he engineered his life so that he could sit quietly and marvel at the minarets, museums and ruins located in his memory, which was still rooted in ravishing Mogadishu, Somalia, even though his body was based in Peckham, South London.

Kayd lived next door to me, and in the first three years that we lived opposite each other I never once invited him over for tea or coffee or conversation. I was wary of him because he was too much like me: too gay, too Somali, too Muslim. Disassociation, fear and straight-up self-loathing often lead to base assessments into which one's cynicism seeps like oil through a bed of leaves.

I initially couldn't see the value of this man. He was my mirror and I refused to acknowledge my reflection. And Kayd never sought my companionship, never asked for help even though I knew he didn't have a support system. My father once said that when the Somali civil war broke out in the nineties, it was as if the whole country and its citizens exhaled and collapsed into a decades-long psychosis that shows no sign of abating. So we circle the globe, settling in Minnesota and Mumbai and Mombasa, in an attempt to shake off our stigmatised shadows, failing to realise that a shadow cannot be shed.

I thought I was inured to this psychology until Kayd showed me that our bilateral interior warscape was in fact an heirloom.

*

'I am not your saviour,' said Kayd.

'I didn't say you were.' I was standing outside his flat, holding out a box of Godiva chocolates.

'Then what is this?' he said, motioning to the chocolates. 'I am not your saviour and a box of rutti-tutti cioccolato ain't going to change that fact. So what do you want?'

'Weed.'

He gave me a look that said, 'I know this negro did not just ask me for some goddam weed,' before slamming the door in my face.

'I'm not leaving this spot,' I said, raising my voice. 'What happened to neighbourliness?'

Kayd opened the door. 'What's my last name?'

'Uh, is this a trick question?' I said.

'No, it's a simple one. What's my last name?'

'Umm...'

'C'mon,' said Kayd, 'you were the one blathering on about neighbourliness. So go on. If you're such a good neighbour, then not only should you know my last name but the last names of my two cats.'

'You have cats?'

'Goodbye, Migil,' said Kayd.

I shoved my foot in his doorway to prevent the door from closing. 'Look,' I said, 'my dealer is out on a date and I could really use a likkle help over here. From one gay Somali brother to another.'

'God, you've got cheek,' chuckled Kayd. 'Wake up and smell the shit-storm, kid. It ain't cute to out a grown man who's simply trying to mind his business for some fricking chamba. Where on earth did you get this entitlement from? Did nobody ever tell thee thou wast wrong once while you was growing up? Jeez.'

'So are you going to hook a brother up or what?'

'Give me those chocolates,' he said. I swiftly handed them over. He inspected the box like a jeweller looking for defects on a diamond. 'Wait here.'

He closed the door. I could hear a whole heap of clattering and cussing. After five long minutes, he opened it again slightly and held out three giant joints.

'Listen, you will be tempted to blaze this shit up in one go. Do not do this. Pace yourself to get that nice fade. This shit is Turkish noise and it will fuck you up right into next Friday, and have you out here looking like a crack whore.'

'Is it crack?' I said.

'Migil, don't make me box you. Here, take this shit and don't disturb my groove again. Comprende?'

'Loud and clear, hombre,' I said, taking the blunts. 'Gracias.'

He grunted and closed the door.

*

Reader, ride with me as I take a small detour. What does success mean to you? Does it mean a bigger house, a sexy partner, some cute kids of your own, a criss car tossed into the stew for added spice? Does success mean more money, a crazy-bangable body or does it signify social clout? What does success – in all its modern iterations – mean to you, reader?

For me, success is something as simple and banal as getting out of bed in the morning. Success is time spent away from the gadgets that act as an enchanted looking glass showing all the harrowing ways mandem were breaking the planet into pieces with hate crimes, climate change denialism, anti-vaccination claptrap, nationalist nonsense and-and-and. All of this is my way of saying that success, for me at least, is peace of mind: the joy of sleeping right at night. This is where weed comes in.

I wanted to smoke myself into the next century.

Sensimilla was a sweetener to counteract the acridity of daily living, which, after Brexit, had the bitter taste of an era-defining anxiety dream. After Boris Johnson was elected into government, I found it harder and harder to reconcile the black rage I felt with my unreality: the black rage and the black blues and black toil of my people, who had fought and died to live in a country that consistently spat in our faces by creating movements to make us feel less welcome, smaller, meaningless.

So I smoked and sexed my way to a semi-sane existence. After I had coaxed Kayd to share some of his Turkish 'delights' with me, I sparked up and spun some Verve remixes of Billie-and-Ella-and-Nina. Soon my arse was suitably skeed and skeezy. I whipped out my silent weapon: a fourteen-inch titanium vibrator that stretched me out and made me sing sonatas, much to the chagrin of my neighbours. I'm happy to report, dear reader, that ho-ism has cleared my skin and made me happier than a pig in muck. This is highness and heat as dawa for a mind in need of healing.

What about Kayd, you ask? What became of him, you wonder, before I took you on this long-winded detour? Don't worry. Kayd is probably doing the exact same thing I'm doing right now in his own apartment: getting blunted on reality and boning himself all the way to a small stroke. We'll check on him in two ticks because this story is about to get weird and wonderful chop-chop. We're about to bring Somali-style matharau to this motherfucker.

*

When I wasn't working as the assistant editor of an online magazine or as the assistant manager of a clothes shop, I hosted a club night in Peckham called Anima Kingdom. I had felt so disheartened by the lack of spaces for femme black blokes that I created a place where once a month fabulous queens and their admirers could come together, drink, dance, snort substances, fuck and essentially be free for a few hours. There was no judgement at the Anima Kingdom and we all got loose and lighter than thistledown.

This was an opportunity for performativity and potent blacketty-black-blackness. The club night became a haven for men both young and old who were coming into their own, flexing their femininity and paying homage to their respective cultures. So the Somali brothers wore dirac, sheer dresses embroidered with mermaids and honeysuckle, their hands adorned with henna filigrees, lips painted the colour of coral stones. The Nigerian bredrin came draped in gold and lace wedding gowns, and my Jamaican brothers rocked quadrille skirts accented with platform boots and bomb beads. It was pure cultural pluralism and everybody served it up straight, no chaser.

One night, whilst I was busy welcoming my guests, I saw a stunning older Somali man dressed in a guntino, toned arms shimmering with glitter, lips lined with gloss. He looked familiar.

'Shit, Kayd?' I said. 'You look fantastic. What happened to you being a hermit?'

He laughed. 'Even the most introverted puto needs to let his peen breathe sometimes. Besides, I heard you have a fantastic DJ and I came to show these young guns how the real OGs get down.'

'Please let me know if you need anything.'

'This ain't my first rodeo, kid,' he smiled.

After all the guests had gone inside the club, I began the proceedings by ripping the microphone and saying, 'Brothers and sistas, brothers and sistas, let us bless this room. During this time of tremendous challenges facing our global community, let us revolt by dancing to the tune of our own riddims. Let us create joyful vibrations and flavour and bounce. DJ Afrodeesia, drop the beat so that all these beauties can shake what the good lord gave them. Hit me.'

DJ Afrodeesia, a striking dreadlocked brother of Greek and Nigerian descent, instantly brought nothing but heat: Destiny's Child singing syncopated songs to the drums of Tony Allen, FKA twigs cooing on a baile funk bassline, Oumou Sangare's voice synced up to Snoop Dogg's 'Beautiful', Cesária Évora's gorgeous paeans over a Pharcyde flex. We danced and offered our dreams up to Olorun, the Sky Father, as the night and our queer black bodies trans-fused into each other.

I was gyrating against a Jamaican stud, buzzing out of my brain, when Kayd interrupted our dance in order to take his place. I turned around and faced tall, mysterious Kayd as he grabbed my waist and ground his hips against mine. I reached for his buttocks and pressed him against me.

He wasn't wearing any underwear under his dress and his derrière had the suppleness of someone who drank milk and did yoga on a daily basis. I kissed him and his tongue tasted of smoke and strawberry bubblegum. He tasted sumptuous and he smelled of oud. I wanted to fuck him right there on the dance floor.

'You're a good kisser,' he said, grinning. 'Now I know why you're such a heartbreaker.'

I laughed. 'You're not bad yourself. How about we grab some smoked ribs and a bottle of brandy after this night is over and enjoy ourselves back home?'

He chuckled and hugged me. 'Beautiful Migil, where have you been all my life?'

'Next door.'

He laughed again and we continued grinding as if the world was ours, as if the past few years of social anxiety and unrest meant nothing. We were here, two Somali men of different generations, singing the hymn of our shared heritage. There is nothing sexier, more sacrosanct, than black courtship. Reader, this connective tissue is how our relationship took on new dimensions.

*

We returned to our block at dawn. Kayd took me by the hand and led me to his apartment. It smelled of mango mist and frankincense. It was the smell of comfort, the site of love, Somalinimo.

The morning winter sky was smudged a pigeon-grey. Kayd lit candles as if he was ushering me into communion. Once the candles were lit, he pressed play on his iPod, which was plugged into a sound system, and out poured the molasses-sweet tone of Melody Gardot. Kayd walked towards me and carefully unwrapped his guntino. The dress fell to the floor and I marvelled at his magnificence. His body was toned, abs gleaming with sweat and cocoa butter, a silver navel ring glinting in the candlelight. He was smooth and silken, dick long and gorgeous. The man's body was godlike and I wanted to worship at his feet.

He kissed me on my forehead, my shoulders, my neck and my lips. He then turned me around, unzipped my dress and laid me down on the sofa, my stilettos sparkling like they were embossed with gold leaf. I tried to take them off but Kayd told me to keep them on. I was on my back. He sucked my nipples, slithered his tongue down my belly until he reached my groin. He blew me until my thighs trembled, until his mouth was glazed with silk thread. He didn't spit.

By now his own dick was dribbling. He unwrapped a condom, rolled it down his rigid cock, lubricated both of us as we caught the most soul-satisfying strokes. He fucked and fucked and fucked me until our bodies were lustrous with sweat, until the room stank of sex and sticky-icky, until we both cried out to the creator. After we had simultaneously climaxed, we lay on the couch in silence, savouring the sixir we had just conjured. It was queer black love as medicine and soft magic, queer black vulnerability as grace and holistic humanism, queer black sex as sensory dynamism and divine ritual. We drank each other in and did it again and again until we were both brimming with pleasure, until we collapsed in each other's arms and dove into dreamless sleep.

*

I woke up earlier than Kayd, who by the way, beloved reader, makes no sound whatsoever when he's snoozing. I got up, groggy and strung out, and took a cursory glance at his living room. Beads and brocaded silk cluttered his desk, next to a neon-green Singer sewing machine, needles, rolls of thread and tubes of silk paint. Hanging above his desk was a mood-board with cut-out photos from fashion magazines like *Dazed, Wonderland* and *i-D*. Alongside these images were crude drawings of designs and patterns. Was Kayd a fashion designer? He had been my neighbour for three years and we didn't know anything about each other, except that we were both gay, Somali, solitary, and smoked a lot. I totted it up to the insane isolation of London living, whereby if quality of life didn't possess the texture of an endurance test, then it was probably as worthless as a pork pie at a Muslim picnic. I didn't know what had made Kayd so hermitic. I didn't know if he was suffering from mental ill-health like me, or if he had any family at all. As I stared at him, sleeping naked on his tatty couch, looking incredibly fragile despite his firm musculature, I knew this man had been hurt so profoundly that his wounds would never fully heal. I got dressed, kissed him on the cheek, and quietly left his apartment.

I went for a walk in the freezing February afternoon to fight ghosts. Why was I doing this? Why was I hooking up with my neighbour, who was more than twice my age? Was my romantic entanglement misplaced desire, a curative for loneliness or a displacement activity with potentially damaging consequences? What was I hoping to gain from this?

A small voice in my head said, 'It's okay to want to be wanted.'

I tried to hold on to this commonsensical approach like a raft, but when your whole life has been a morass of self-doubt and destructive behaviour, it's difficult to school yourself on the basic tenets of being a halfway well-adjusted human. I was a mess, reader. The voice in my head came through once again and said, 'Take it slowly. You don't have to slit your wrists to see sense. Enjoy this moment because that's all life is: a series of disjointed moments that may eventually coalesce into a semi-comprehensible whole.'

As I traipsed down Rye Lane trying to quell the riot within, I realised that all of this was transitory: the distress, the blueness of my imagination. It was all cyclical and my survival hinged on this understanding. I was unanchored right now, but this moment would soon segue into a sense of rootedness. Dispiritedness and anxiety were not fertile soil for a new relationship to bloom in, but if I tended it with care and patience, then I would reap wonders. I popped into my favourite restaurant, Tupi, which served massive portions of

Brazilian dishes. I ordered dill infused salmon and poached eggs with hollandaise sauce along with sweet potato rosti with avocado and kale drizzled with chilli butter. I ordered to go and rushed back home.

When I got into my house, I put the food on a tray and shoved it in the oven to keep warm. I set the dining table whilst jamming to a soundtrack of sun-soaked funk. When that was done, I walked over to Kayd's apartment and rang the buzzer. I heard him grunting and knocking things over before finally opening the door. His eyes were bloodshot and his mouth was smeared with dried drool, lip gloss and glitter.

'I got lunch,' I said, 'so get your cute ass over to mine.'

'What are you, some woodland sprite?' he groaned. 'How are you so energetic after the night we've had?'

'Oh, trust me, honey, I've already had my mid-afternoon meltdown. So I'll see you in two?'

'I stink of sex and sweat,' he said, 'I'mma need more than two minutes to freshen up.'

'Just put on a dressing gown.'

'Okay, let me brush at least.'

'And bring some weed,' I said.

'Man, I thought you were using me for my dope body, not my dope.'

'Can't it be both?' I smiled, kissing him. He tasted of me.

'It's a good thing you're a great kisser.'

I laughed and went back to my house, leaving the door unlocked for him.

He came in ten minutes later and took in the décor: the

butterfly magnets covering the red fridge, the Disney and Star Wars mugs on the shelf, the bottles and bottles of perfume arranged on my dressing table, mementos from former lovers who no longer mattered. My apartment was a studio, much smaller than his two-bedroom digs. After surveying it, he said, 'I like this place a lot. What's that incense you're burning? It smells wonderful.'

'It's called Badu's Pussy,' I smiled.

'Her cooch is clearly popping. Shit, that smells good. Makes me want to wife you up right now.'

I laughed and told him to sit at the table as I removed the food from the oven and served it to him. As he ate, he moaned like he was having the most life-affirming orgasm. After we finished eating, he rolled us some sensi and we smoked in silence, two soul-brothers meditating on the strange journey that had brought us together; the spiritual properties of coitus, kindness and ice-cool symbiosis.

'So you're a club promoter,' said Kayd.

'Amongst other things. And you're a fashion designer, I take it.'

He didn't say anything for a second. 'My mother was a tailor in Mogadishu. Her designs were sculptural, exquisitely crafted. She made her customers – all of them wealthy birds – look like Nefertiti.' He blazed, then ground the joint out in the ashtray. 'She died during the civil war. She was in our back garden, purifying herself for prayer when she caught a stray bullet. I never got over it. She had raised us. She was an old woman when she was killed.'

'Samir iyo imaan,' I said quietly.

'I was here in London, having sex with a stranger when my family called to tell me the news. I couldn't travel to Somalia for the funeral because there were no flights to Mogadishu.'

He wiped his eyes. 'I make clothes in order to stay connected to her. She taught me everything about design. This life is cruel, kid.'

'Is that why you keep to yourself?' I asked.

'Never allow yourself to be ravaged by grief.'

He got up to leave. I grabbed his hand, pulled him to me and gave him a warm hug.

'Stay,' I said.

'I will only disappoint you.'

'I will honour you if you meet me halfway,' I said.

'I can't,' he said, breaking the embrace and leaving my apartment.

I didn't go after him.

*

Reader, there's no compass to map a complicated man's emotional terrain. I wanted to love up on Kayd but his pain was deeper than the Danube. I hadn't lost a parent like he had. I hadn't been disowned by my family due to my sexuality. In fact, my parents were loving and queerer than the late and legendary Pepper Labeija. I was privileged as a gay black bloke in a predominantly white, increasingly racist country because I was insulated from the harsh experiences faced by most folks of colour across the spectrum. Mi familia was black and queer, my doctor was black and queer, my psychiatrist was black and queer, my local police officer was black and queer, my bosses were black and queer, my friends were black and queer. Homogeneity in Brexit-era England was increasingly not remarkable, as most motherfuckers and they mamas careened towards separatism, but I was protected from the worst prejudices.

My longwinded point is I empathised with Kayd but I couldn't imagine the ostracism and sorrow he felt. My parents, who were only slightly younger than him, and more directly connected to the times of the Civil War, could understand his anguish, but it was a foreign language to me. So I did what I was taught to do in moments where misperception threatened: I laid down my arms and tried to move like a conservationist tending to a wounded deer, which is to say, I tried to move with compassion.

Later that evening, I met up with my Aabo at John the Unicorn, a gay gastropub on Rye Lane. We ordered vodka on the rocks and chopped it up.

'Aabo, I know your relationship with your parents was difficult, but do you ever feel guilty for icing them out?'

'No,' said Aabo, sipping his vodka. 'I didn't reject my parents and neither did your mum. My father, your awoowe, was a hardass. When I came out to him, he dismissed me and I had to make a decision: stay tethered to a toxic situation out of filial duty or fuck off. I chose to fuck off for the sake of my sanity. I've told you this before but there's a history of madness in my family, which is where your mental health woes stem from: that shizz is hereditary. But I don't know anyone from our community who isn't caught up in the quagmire of psychic damage. We dress it up, perfume that mierda, say our prayers, medicalise religion. But religion, like all medicine, offers only half the answers. The rest is down to exercise, emotional hygiene, decent diet and sleep, companionship, effort.' My Aabo sighed. 'These aren't things that come naturally to everyone. It takes years and years of perseverance. How could it not? Instead, I directed all my energy towards you, your Hooyo, your Adeer, your Habo. I'm a postman. The pay is shit. The work is not stimulating but I'm successful. I have a loving, stable family life. When I go to bed at night, I sleep like a newborn. If everything else must go, then so be it. But peace? Pop that mambo straight into my veins.'

'What I should do about Kayd?' I said.

'You had a one-night stand with your neighbour. Stop sweatin' bullets. This Kayd character has baggage. How could he not? You don't get to be a grown man without some painful memories. I'm proud of you, son. You're opening yourself up to the possibility of love.'

'Aabo, I don't know if I'll ever be ready for love,' I said.

My Aabo sipped his vodka again. 'I can't think of anyone who's more nurturing than you. Let me tell you something about love. When you meet your person, there's no second guessing. You will find that love is easy, unlike everything we've been taught by the romance industrial complex. You will know when you meet your twin flame and I don't think you should compromise until then.'

I knew that sadness swam through the eyes of the lonely, and that each failed relationship intensified one's inability to love more openly. It was learned behaviour and depression that had dyed all my dreams a murky tincture.

My Aabo and I left the bar at closing time and went for a walk around Peckham. The air was cold, but crisp and clear. We strolled down Rye Lane with its recent avalanche of expensive restaurants and bars. My Aabo and I were witnesses to a neighbourhood in transition, a neighbourhood that was once so proudly black African you had to double-check to see whether you had inadvertently travelled to the slums of Kinshasa or Lagos, that was now a neighbourhood too expensive for even entry-level bankers to live in unless they had social housing or a family hand-up. And yet gentrification meant that my entire world was now located in this district: my jobs, my social life, my family, my friends. I hadn't travelled into Central London for almost six months because everything was right here on my doorstep.

As we turned into Choumert Grove, the posters promoting my club night, Anima Kingdom, which featured my dolled-up face in high definition, were pasted on the walls. Some scallywag had taken a neon-pink spray can to my lips and graffitied the following on there:

'This bitch knows how to bring the heat. I can't take this ho!!!!!!!!!'

My Aabo and I burst into drunken giggles. We laughed and laughed and laughed. Afterwards, Aabo gave me a kiss on the forehead and said, 'I'm proud of you.'

*

When I came home, I found a package sitting on the mat outside my door. It was wrapped in purple paper. I picked it up, went in and opened it greedily. Maybe it was a present from my Hooyo (who had hinted that she would bequeath her blood-stone necklace to me at some point. Maybe the moment had arrived – though surely she wouldn't leave something of such value on the doorstep). Instead it was a box of Godiva choco-lates, three giant joints and a small, perfumed card that read:

'I will honour you by meeting you halfway. (By the way, don't smoke the enclosed in a rush. You will feel like your sexy ass has skyrocketed to Mars).'

Reader, my heart did a pirouette. I grabbed my keys and headed for the door so I could go over to Kayd's crib and lace him with some lip-smacking Sauce-N-Stroke. When I opened my door, he was standing outside, smiling. I kissed him for what seemed like a thousand years.

'Come inside.'

THE NECKINGER LINE

SWITHUN COOPER

Night. You lean against the wharf's black railings and stare at the Victorian warehouse on the dock. Its brickwork looks shabby now – squat and coarse against the glass precision of the new offices behind it. But the stink in the air, the stink of salt and dirt, is the same, and it still means sex to you. This is your old haunt: Southwark's tip, where the Thames runs low and opens to the mouth of the underground river.

He strides towards you. The wind lifts, tightening the cold skin on your cheekbones.

You agreed to join him here as part of a tour group. They left an hour ago. Since then he's filled your phone with messages: apologies, hints, the power-play of flirtation. You wouldn't leave without letting me find out what you bleed like. Sorry, is that too much, haha.

Thanks for waiting, he says, oh fuck, I'm even later than I thought, work was manic.

You smile and tell him: An hour, that's no time at all.

Let's set off anyway, he says, you know the route already, right? And they can't have gone far with all that history to learn beforehand. I bet we'll catch them up before the first pair of trousers even drops to the ankles.

You head south with him. These roads have been widened since you walked them last. They are soaked with white street light and so are the alcoves and passages. He puts on the clammy voice of a courtroom judge: Eliminate the shadows! he says. Without hiding places to fuck they'll die out or turn straight! He brings his body close as he speaks, then slides a hand inside your coat. Deftly he twists a button off your shirt. His fingertips press and pinch the skin on your chest. He's feeling it out, you understand – he wants it confirmed that you really have no heartbeat. In the full light of the street you pause. You say: Go on. Press again. Press harder.

*

You were talking with him on the app, arranging to meet, when you told him about your heart. Full disclosure, you said, and explained how it stopped one day but you kept on going: you've been twenty-two years old for centuries. You waited for him to block you or ask is this roleplay? But instead he sent you an image for an event. WE'RE HISTORY! it said. QUEER WALKING TOUR WITH ALL-GENDER IMMERSIVE CRUISING! It's invite-only, he added, we're going to reclaim the past, learn about the cruising spots of old, and fuck them back into existence. You can tell me afterwards what the tour guide got wrong.

You looked at the route the image proposed. The Neck-inger, where cargo came for the tanneries, where the milliners stretched their fabrics in the open, where you waited on that warehouse dock until someone gave you the nod to follow. The feel of damp soot on your hands and chin as you held yourself to the smeary black walls for men. Men who shared your language or didn't, men who worked on the boats or owned them. Arousal came like nausea as you recalled the gassy scent of bodies and mud. You'd almost forgotten you ever knew it.

Looks fun, you answered. Meet you there.

*

His tongue on your neck now, just below your ear. When he pulls away there is colour in his cheeks. He puts a thumb to your wrist and feels for a pulse, then something passes across his face – a ripple of shame, it looks like. He lets go.

We should catch them up, he says.

He walks fast. You have to run to get back alongside him. On the corner you catch his arm and gesture; beside the doorway to a community garden a foil square lies torn on a paving slab. It's too clean to be from anything but this evening. They've started, he says, and hustles you inside.

What was this garden before? You aren't sure. Perhaps it wasn't anything – just private space behind a wall you never scaled. You cross the grass and he follows, glancing around, but the tour has passed on already. The barest smell of sweat. Two condoms, wrinkling in the soil of the border.

He turns back to the door. Don't, you say. You open your coat to show the skin where your missing button makes the shirt gape. He comes close, smiles, undoes the others. The cold air on your skin makes you instantly hard.

He unbuttons his fly and lifts his T-shirt. His belly is a firm mound with rough yellow hairs. Facing you he takes your wrist again – his thumb against the place where your pulse isn't – and slides your hand inside his underwear. Gently he moves your fingers into his cunt. He guides you, rubbing slowly faster, and you watch him realise how much you like being instructed. Suddenly he lifts your hand out and pushes your fingers, wet, deep into your mouth.

Turn round, he says, and you obey. He cups his palm to the back of your skull. Trailing ivy covers the nearest wall and he pushes your face against it. Drop your arms, he says, and he pulls off your coat, yanks your trousers and underwear to your thighs. Kneeling behind you he shifts your legs apart. You let out a pale gasp of joy as you feel his beard on your skin and his tongue inside you. He bends his neck, then, and bites you hard on the inside thigh. Traffic screams on the other side of the wall.

*

He holds your coat while you button your shirt. Again his manner has dulled to awkwardness. When he speaks his voice has a desperate strain, as if he's saved it from falling into a pit.

Well, he says. Was that like old times?

You shake your head. Perhaps others fucked here. I never did.

So we're making history, then.

Lifting your coat, he helps you into it. Sorry, he says. With the teeth. I got carried away.

Not enough, you tell him. We'll need to work harder to break the skin, next time.

He blushes and you nudge him to get walking. By now the tour will have reached the mills or the cemetery. You realise the cemetery might no longer be there, and if it is, all the best fucking spots might be lost. In which case the group will be further on: you picture them tucked in the doorways of pubs, decoding the names. The William Sikes, The Rookery. Would it be better to catch them up, and let this conflict he clearly feels about you – fascinated, aroused, then suddenly troubled – play out in company? He might be more encouraged, more likely to take what he wants, less likely for his desire to turn him against you.

But you like it that the two of you are alone.

Stepping back into the street light you see the knees of his grey denim trousers, grubby from the earth and grass he knelt on. You think of your own dirt, your own markings and scars. You tell him: Listen. You're not the first to be intrigued by how I bleed.

He nods, unsure.

If you're worried about what it means, to use me like that –

He winces. Your breath catches as you say: There's some-where we can go. Private. If you want.

*

You're off the path of the Neckinger now. The old industrial area: factories, large, flecked buildings with high windows, spiked metal fences in front of railway arches. The storehouses you briefly worked in are now distilleries and breweries. There is no romance here, no air of spit and gristle – just the dull, threaded sky and the winking lights of the nearby high-rise flats.

Where are we? he asks. What used to happen here?

Everywhere's a cruising spot if you use it right, you tell him. It's not what the tour would call real history. Just mine.

To your left a dirt track with stagnant puddles from yesterday's rain. When the Neckinger was built over, when the wharf's warehouses closed and you slipped between labour and trade as time required, you would huddle beneath the awning here and smoke cigarettes, waiting for the men coming off their factory shifts.

You walk down the track and indicate a corner, out of sight of the main street, but he stays at the lip of the alley. Is he afraid? Does he think, perhaps, it is you who will hurt him? You think of the image he sent: IMMERSIVE CRUISING. Not cruising as you knew it, but as play. Risk like a fantasy, infusing the mind, but not as an actual threat to the body. Like your heart. You told him and he grew instantly excited. But here at the line where it becomes reality, where it moves from a message he sends to an act he commits – this is the line that troubles him.

Oh, you say. Oh. Let me show you.

Slowly, beneath the awning, you undress. You fold your clothes on the floor and stand, naked, still at a distance from him. The hair on your body prickles and your nipples pinch pleasurably. You shiver.

Only he can see you here. There is no desire to be witnessed by anyone but him. There is no desire for anything except for him to tell you what to do – to dress or stay naked, to kneel, to move, to bleed. Can he tell this about you? Are you making it clear?

He steps towards you, slips his own clothes off. You take his hand and look at the nail on his index finger: not long, but long enough. You bite its corner, snapping it to make a sharp edge. You draw the point down your forearm. It scrapes the skin but does not break it, yet.

Can I? he asks.

Yes, you tell him. Anywhere.

He places his hand on your chest and looks in your eyes. You nod. You have to keep telling him: harder, harder. Sweat breaks out on his forehead, his eyes narrow, and at last the thin blade of his nail goes in. He drags it with effort over your heart. A line where the skin splits.

Wow, he says.

You nod. No heartbeat, you say, no pulse. Nothing to make it flow out.

You can feel his awe as he puts his palms on your chest, either side of the cut, and nudges. Your blood hangs just beneath the surface. He lets go. It retreats. He is in total control.

He turns you around, his stomach on the small of your back. From behind he puts his fingers to your hipbone. This is when your blood is least still: it's down in your cock, which throbs. The tip stings. His hand goes around it, his thumb traces the long vein. His other hand runs from your shoulder blade to your flank, feeling out the scars other men have made.

You're close, you're so close. You hope he makes you wait.

*

There have been men who fuck you like they're trying to jumpstart you. As if it's a reflection on them – a test of their virility to get your heart beating. Men who ask questions, over and over. What was it like when your heart stopped? When did you realise you weren't ageing? Do you miss having a pulse? Exhausting to keep explaining, like a representative of some small nation: Yes, I am human, but an uncommon one. What is normal about the body is not always what is natural, or necessary.

And men for whom your heart means you slip out of reality for them. They fuck you like they're the only ones having sex, and you are there to make it happen. They move you around, give you bruises and welts, cut you for the sight of it. They make you stand while they watch you heal. They forget it is your experience, not just theirs.

And at the centre of this, the problem. Something you can't get right in your mind. These men use you. Yet you crave this use. That moment just before a man cuts you is when you feel most scared and most excited. Did this desire stem from the way you've been treated? Is it like the docks and the wharf – which were, for so long, your only opportunities for fucking that they shaped how you came to understand it? Or is it a coincidence: you like being used, and this is how it tends to happen for you.

It can make you feel like a visitor in your own body, or like you're watching it from a distance. The best way you know to get your blood moving, to return to yourself, is to return to this line. This boundary of risk and reality.

*

Before pulling on his own clothes, he lifts your shirt and hands it to you. Taking it you catch the orange street light from over the wall, and he sees the cut you both made on your chest. Parted skin, entirely bloodless.

Oh, he says.

Well, you explain, it all went south. You point to your fading erection and he smirks.

The two of you locate the river's path. You cross through housing estates with strong red brickwork, admire the warped glass panels of their stairwells. You hear the rush of water and realise you've reached the bridge across the dock where the Neckinger once re-entered the Thames.

Look, he says.

Along the wharf, in small dark edges, the tour group. Some are on their knees and some stand together, moving to each other's rhythms. Nearest to you a woman peels back her jacket, and a shaven-headed figure presses hungrily against her, mouth to chest.

We never fucked here, you say.

It's historical reenactment, he says. Not historical repetition.

You place your hands on the wall of the bridge.

Really? he says. It's a main road.

You nod at the dock and say: We can go among them.

Yes, he whispers, then: No.

Still at your side he checks his sharpened nail and then selects a different finger. Reaching behind, he slides it discreetly into you, and you imagine what this might look like: the muscle clenched in the dark, your veins slow or still. His left hand moves down past your navel and strokes you. The blood again, the throbbing. This man, you think: right now he knows the line. The tip of your cock is wet, then so is his hand, and he lifts his dripping palm to your mouth. You swallow.

In the near dark, involuntary groans, caught breath. The creaking dock. It did not often happen this way, you think, not at the time. But it is happening this way now.

LIPOPHILIC, MALLEABLE SOLIDS NEAR AMBIENT TEMPERATURES

NICKS WALKER

If ever asked do you have a partner? Would you be interested in fucking me/him/us? he would always answer, ever so graciously 'I was done with living boys by the time I was sixteen, my love.'

His voice was warm and tonic, like honey and lemon on a sore throat, and it helped the words pass over his lips and glide down without a fight. Usually, it got a small laugh – nervous, or otherwise.

It was true. And in the museum-bleached shadow of a colossal marble man, with a penis arching well over his shoulder and a cocktail in his hand, who could blame him? He stood in the shadows of the gods, always looking up.

He was an artist first and critic second – or maybe a critic first, and an artist after all. One certainly helped him get away with the other, but which had come first was lost to history. If asked, did chickens lay eggs or eggs lay chickens, he'd have laughed and told you if you wanted to make it in the arts, you should leave the hens alone and find a wealthy cock. But whether he had daddy's money or Daddy's money was equally unclear. He seemed unruffled by any indignity, and he luxuriated in filth.

All that was really known about his finances was that he'd kept the house out of the twitching fingers of the National Trust.

The house (he rejected any nicknames out of hand, calling the place 'as yet Untitled') was a sprawl. It was listed beyond belief, in a state of peri-collapse, and he kept it just so, employing only the most bloody-minded and difficult-to-work-with specialists to touch up the gold finishings and restructure the crumbling plaster. The purpose of the house was not to be a house – it was to be an object, a meta object, a decorative arse encompassing his private mausoleum of cock.

He was a creator and a collector – perhaps the foremost curator – of gay erotic statue. The house was a hedge-maze, drawing visitors deeper and tighter into his world in gradual, well-lubricated inches.

The gardens (meticulously overgrown) were full of figures running, playing – pert arses poking out of bushes that had been carved into enormous penises, veined with ivy. Wild-eyed Satyrs and Pan figures running, erections in paws. Others, Satan figures, sat with legs spread, inviting, on benches that had occasionally been nicked in the night from a local park. Couples copulated in the undergrowth, legs tangled unselfconsciously over the path for visitors to trip over. Male figures lingered by the pond in the manner of Hampstead Heath, an eternal postcard. (One stared, dead-eyed, up from the bottom of the pool).

Inside the house, rooms were subdivided into themes, acts, some taken up by whole interconnected orgies. The bath was filled by a haberdashery of pissing male nudes, the toilet a series of open-mouthed angels, the shower was a genuine logistical marvel. The kitchen worktop balanced on the arse-cheeks and shoulders of two muscular Atlases, locked in an eternal 69.

But the heart of his work, his collection, lined the corridors leading to the master bedroom. Prized among these – his lovers – were a selection of cocks commissioned by a friend, inspired by the great nudes of history. One of his favourites, *the origin of the world*, imagined Courbet's spread, hairy cunt as a stout, thick penis resting on a heavy set of balls. He had Michelangelo's David, obviously, while God and Adam reached towards each other like lovers spilling out of tight leather trousers in the piss-sticky haze of a 1970s public bathroom. Venus, reborn, was short, soft and unerect – for soft-softly licking and taking into his mouth.

In this part of the collection, there were only two cunts: one, a display piece in granite, was made by and in honour of his first and final boyfriend. Like almost all of his statues, it was both self-satire and a kind of queer transcendence: no one could ever penetrate a stone cunt.

The other, his own cunt, he had poured in bronze so that time could show where he had gently (vigorously) touched it

– testosterone-heavy clitoris rubbed green with overuse, like his own. It hung superimposed over the face of the cartoonishly endowed and erect Satan figure he most liked to take into his 'Virgin Cunt', positioned such that he could eat it out – eat himself out – while he fucked himself on the devil's dick.

He had outgrown living boys long, long ago.

He was aware he was making love to a mirror: something frozen, incapable of reciprocation. But it felt more like carving the motions of his sex into the marble of entropy. Sculpting felt like tugging away the dirt and rock, like erosion forms a cave. He was fingering open that cave, his chisel was the lube-slicked digits of the Goddess. He had a talent for form unmatched by anyone in his generation, so much so that society simply had to take his subject matter and swallow it – like cough syrup, LSD, or cum. Curating, then, was like moving mountains. He was an artist and a curator. The cock and balls of art were object and context, made one whole in juxtaposition.

Did he feel attracted to the statues he made? asked some sweat-stained *Guardian* reporter. He had laughed – who isn't making art to fuck?

But he was an invert (he had always enjoyed that term): fucking art, not being fucked because of it. He was not to be consumed – he was consumable, made eternal by existing with one clear narrative purpose, and denying it. He had been desired, reviled, rejected, lusted for, fantasised about. Seductive, but never seduced. Consumability was one of his few coping mechanisms for mortality, and he wasn't about to give in, having made it firmly into the handsome consolidation and decline of his late fifties unmoved. His cock, barely seen, barely touched, and unable to produce cum, loomed permanently erect over the shoulder of (art) history.

He made love only to unrealities, to dreams, and to mirrors.

It was the friend who had forged *the origin of the world* who had told him about the collection. It had appeared in a recent issue of *Raw Vision*, a retrospective on the Society of the Eternal Wax, a small group of occultists who fled from the Weimar Republic just as the jackboot landed, crunching, on the fragile neck of a fledgling queer utopia. They had squatted a failed wool and/or hunting estate in the western edges of the Highlands, with just enough neighbours that stories of nudity, sodomy, whippings, animist rituals and other such party familiars began to slowly trickle out. People who really minded were, thankfully, just a little bit more than a burning torch's walk away.

Then, as quickly as they had arrived, they had disappeared, leaving only a building full of wax figurines, strict instructions for the upkeep of the estate, and a heavy chest full of gold. The son of the son of the groundskeeper, a pheasant beater they had kept on to trim the hedges and know about sheep, kept the land now. Apparently in accordance with the strict instructions of the long-dead magicians, in exchange for a salary in gold, set out in what claimed to be an eternal contract.

He had started booking the train somewhere around *animist rituals*.

The groundskeeper, Angus, was a handsome man, almost non-verbal, and bright behind the eyes. He seemed as accustomed to art-folk as sheep, and regarded them with a similar pleasant, slightly paternalistic condescension. The rules, as they applied to visitors, were simple: have a look, touch nothing, and do try to get out before the sun starts to set in the Temple.

He stepped through the grand, slightly tattered double doors and felt his heart – felt it, so present in his chest, a fragile handful of meat fluttering with all the immortality of a butterfly. The entrance hall was in ruins, and not the careful decay of his own unhome. These were the ruins of a free-party, a rave. Furniture had either been stacked in esoteric ways or smashed against the walls, paintings turned upside down and scrawled over with complex, obscene images several times the height of a man, in what looked like, but surely couldn't be, spray paint.

Hanging by the neck in the middle of the space was a mannequin, with cocks strapped to it at various haphazard angles: from one arse-cheek, two on its chest like tits, and one covering its mouth.

The unexpected time-disclocation of it all was perverse in a way he couldn't have anticipated, and he had to remind himself about the instructions. This was all the well-meaning interpretation of a kindly, ageing heterosexual. This was The Occult, magickal – not magical.

The hanging man swayed with a soft squeaking, coyly revealing that JUDAS had been painted across his other arse-cheek in lipstick. He decided to go directly to the conservatory: he'd arrived late, and this place had no respect for time.

Indeed, it was almost sunset when he picked his way over an upturned oak table – the ruins of a pile of candles scattered on the ground like shrapnel – and into the Temple of the Eternal Wax. This was the heart of the living-dead exhibit.

Stained-glass frescos in the manner of The Stations of the Cross (but featuring mutated human bodies frozen in acts of copulation and mutilation) shone turquoise, red and amber lights over a seething, pooling nightmare of wax. As above, so below: two bodies touching their enormous, swollen genitals leaned towards each other and joined at the head to make one animal, rising up in wax and glass over an orgy in hell itself. Body parts in this world were secondary to acts, to motion. They seemed to emerge, as needed, to perform, and to perform function.

He felt the most compelled, most aroused, he had ever felt in his life – so much so that he was not even surprised to find he was suddenly completely nude. Had he been nude for a while? His clothes weren't around him. Maybe he had taken them off in the hallway, in respect for JUDAS, The Hanged Man.

This seemed right, seemed sensible. Something about the piece was asking that of him, and he was responding.

The room was hot with colour and hot, simply hot. The complex geometry of the frescos focused light in a series of scattered points, like little stars, or flecks of blood. He could feel it on his belly, his labia, the crest of his left knee.

It had to be sunset.

But leaving was not a thing he could imagine doing. Quite literally. It felt like all the heat, the colour, the sex in the universe was here, in this room. Being here, now, felt like drugs, felt like the raw concept of the purest high, like being penetrated by an angel in the biblical sense, a thousand eyes pouring into his arse and cunt.

The heat was melting the wax, he realised.

The heat was animating the wax.

All his life he had carved motion out of stillness, and now he watched stillness becoming motion like a scientist breathing the first gulp of air on Mars.

The slow drizzle of honey, the sprawl of a pile of waking lions, took shape, and the shape it took was one of total, blissfully violent copulation. As the room heated it became an anarchic dance of pure sex, impure sex, bodies growing penetrating parts and grasping parts, fluttering with nodules of pleasure like a genital coral reef. Bodies formed and crashed into one another, wax flesh transcending the boundaries of skin, of organs.

In wax, lovers could become one mind and one body, and one mind (or one body) could become anything.

He stood – did he stand? What were his limbs doing, hands doing?

A body was emerging out of the throbbing mycelium of sex, heavy tits and neat, dripping cunt carved as perfectly in the flowing, pulsing wax as his hands might find them in marble. It turned towards him, mouth forming into an enormous grin, giving itself enough eyes to hold his gaze.

It walked towards him. A candle flickered between them, lit by the burning light of the sunset – the sunset. The perfect sunset, all turquoise and now. Now, a timeless, red now.

He could see two unconnected splashes of wax copulating: what was that, an elbow and a knee? A stomach and a spine? Two clitori docking?

As the figure walked it peeled the tits from its chest and handed them, with care, to figures emerging either side of it, dancing out of the wax pool to race off on giddy adventures into the house, one tit on each, cocks swinging between their legs.

The figure stood over the candle, and gently took his hands. He held them tight.

Holding his gaze like every lover he'd never had it descended, slowly, onto the candle. He went with it, watching as the fire turned the perfectly carved cunt between its legs into a melting stream, a parody of his own, dripping cunt. All features blended away as it got closer, closer, until it touched – extinguishing the flame and bursting, clutching, head tipping back and screaming a silent agony. He clutched too at the wax hands melting softly around his own hands like a drowning man, mouth open, silent, feeling the reverberations of utter, unspeakable pleasure. The figure ground itself into the candle like a breeding animal, rutting, eventually rising, the candle between its legs – a cock. Fused.

He sobbed. Sobbed like a baby. Sobbed for his body, for being touched, for orgasm, for a penis, for eternity. Wax hands were wrapping around his wax hands.

LIPOPHILIC...

He fell forward and he was caught, sex formed a thousand hands to catch him, naked as a dying man. It filled his cunt and his arse and his mouth and his throat, his nose and his ears. And then it was both filling him and he was filling it, he was pushing into it, he was a cock sliding so gentle-tentatively in. They were all the nervous gasp of a sweat-slick virgin, they were all the gentle opening and tightening of a homecoming, they were each other, they were unstoppable, they were forever and ever and ever and ever amen.

They played for eternity. And he is still so, so happy.

CIRCUIT JAM

VIVIEN HOLMES

The sky tonight is full of fires.

It's been 238 days since my husband died. That was 536 days after he was initially diagnosed. 127 days before that, we were sitting on a bench in the lunar observatory – our eighteenth anniversary. The sky looks just like it did that night.

Val calls across to me:

'Kim, how are you doing? You haven't touched your food.'

I think they chose this restaurant because it was one of the few Victor and I hadn't been to together, which is a nice thought, but there's nowhere that doesn't remind me of him still. The way he laughed, the creak of his implants in the rain, the quiet echo of his thoughts running round my head. Feeling that flow of life steadily fade away in the last few days was the worst part of it.

Since Victor's funeral (214 days ago), I've left the house 17 times. Once to stay with Val for a few nights just afterwards, twice briefly to visit my brother, three quiet meals out with friends, six times to the lawyer's offices, four walks out to the forest and once to that place. That's not counting the two months I left the body behind, wandering consciousness through cyberspace mind; my body was still home, I suppose, and what I was doing then isn't comparable to going out to dinner by the canal. I'm calling this number 18 either way.

I met Val and Victor on the same day, my eighth day of university. I noticed them before they noticed me, as anyone would guess. They were loud and almost over-friendly. They'd grown up together in the same neighbourhood, gone to the same school. I'd spent the first ten years of my life in a Hub: a spark of electricity fizzling around, developing moods, interests, a personality, a gender. Eight years of social training and development tweaks later, there I was in the world, confronted by these towering cyborgs, their limbs flitting between fluid and silicon. I'd always been intrigued by people with fixed bodies, having something like a home within themselves. I've inhabited this body for a decade or so now, but it's a different sort of mine.

I try to mention this to Val but it doesn't go well; I trip over my words.

'What are you talking about Kim? I don't really understand.'

'Never mind.'

'Don't say that. I'm here to listen, I want to help.'

Don't we all. Val keeps talking about inner monologues and concepts of thought. It's funny, we're so fascinating to them but it's often unreciprocated. Still, that spark of life in them: seeing it so viscerally in flesh can sometimes, out of the blue, feel so bizarre and beautiful. The first time we met, Victor kept leaning back, his top pulling up and blue streaks rippling over his belly like a thousand tiny fish, and in that moment I was suddenly overwhelmed by this paradoxically awe-inspiring limitation of individuality. That, and lust, I suppose. I can't (shouldn't) discount that intrigue.

Val's skin has a ripple to it today, gentle wanderings like ink through water. I can't concentrate on what either of us are saying, really; my thoughts have been spiralling into spiderwebs lately. It's hard not to wallow in memories. A waiter carrying a mushroom dish goes past. It's what he would have ordered.

Over the first six months, I was transfixed by how Victor just lived, in utter wonder at the depth of his warmth. The look in his eyes and the electric murmur of his skin on the day we connected permanently, as the torrent of his every thought and feeling poured into me. Each pore and each port and each masochistic self-destruction open beyond anything, something more than flowing, more than anything else I'd ever been. That single-mindedness, that limitation.

I relax, fade back into conversation; we chat for 73 minutes, mainly about art, avoiding the topic of Victor. We're both thinking about him though, flickers of a smile or a particular coffee date. Val's latest piece is something durational; they've had a caesium clock installed and everything. Something about distance and information. It's always very impressive when explained in the moment, but I never fully understand what they're getting at.

Afterwards, we walk along the canal, not speaking, just existing alongside each other, thoughts swimming between us. We're better friends now, after spending all that time together by a hospital bed, and the grief afterwards. Streetlights flicker in the water; I clasp Val's hand. They squeeze back. 13 minutes later, I break the silence:

'I'm not sure how to keep doing this. I can still barely do... anything. Just living is such hard work now.'

'These things take time. You'll get through it, you're a very strong person.'

They sound genuine, but platitudes are platitudes.

They walk me back to my flat: one-bed, humanoid-sized, no organic ports required. I'd been so used to living with too-big beds and too-big doors that it took a while to become comfortable there, but it meant there was less to fret about, and there was extra room not taken up by hygiene ports. Small upsides.

In the bedroom, I check over my body, running diagnostics. It's relaxing, the stream of data consistent as always. There's some breaking news alert that I ignore. The air around my body flows and eddies as I open my ports one by one, flushing out the heat and cleaning meticulously. The floor is soft. I focus on the pressure of my body against cool, soft metal. My memory banks clock over. A scrap of skin-mesh flakes off from my left shoulder. On the other side of the house, a tap drips once, then stops. The flake rests on the floor, out of sight, now fully external. They say it's the same with humans and their skin, their stomach biomes: the eternal Ship of Theseus. That poet compared it to some insect – the bagworm – gathering up parts of its shell from its surroundings. There's video of one spinning itself into a cocoon, pine needles here and there. Very cute. I don't know what I'm saying, something like philosophy, or a poem; there's no way of ever being and not, how can you lack what you simply can't have? I'm not designed for thinking like this. I don't know how to be. I should rest.

It is 11pm. The fires in the sky are fading. I am lonely. That seems like something to deal with. Each interaction throws open this feeling of utter emptiness in my everyday, an indication of how I could be, of what it would be like to share my being with someone again. I need more, something powerful, something lasting.

∫

I return back along the canal (number nineteen); there's still a bustle of people here and there, and still hues in the sky. Is this a secret? I haven't told anybody, but I only really speak to Val and we weren't really talking about coping. I think I'm just not mentioning it, not purposefully, not shamefully, but maybe it doesn't have to concern anyone else.

The door is plain, wooden, thick. It's one of the older buildings in the area, 22nd Century probably, one of those neo-Georgian ones. All very pretty. I walk past it. I accidentally turn onto the street where we used to go shopping together, where the old bar was. I turn back immediately and dash past. The door is open now. Someone goes in, I don't see who, but a slime-cyborg, the host, stands on the threshold, beckoning them in, red flesh, shorter and stouter than Victor (no, stop, enough). I wait, watch what happens, and keep going.

Fifth time past. The door is open; the host stands by it again. Nobody is coming in or out. He's noticed me. I stare at his hands, his skinny fingers, his skinny fingers. Victor's were not, they were thick, and long. This isn't him. I walk over. He reaches a hand up to my face and speaks softly, smiling. He has kind eyes.

'Evening b a b y, good to see you finally stop by. What're you h e r e for?'

'Visiting the sauna... Please.'

It's not a real sauna and never has been, too much risk of corrosion with all that humidity. His smile glistens; opal teeth, very fashionable right now. 2864 days ago, Victor gave me an opal necklace that I wore for 1476 days straight, only stopping when it fell in the Cassiopeian sea on an anniversary trip.

'Have you been here b e f o r e?'

'Yes, once.'

'So you know a l l there is to know?'

'I'd say so, yes.'

'Welcome to the house, f r i e n d.'

He leads me down the stairs, one arm stretching round me and gliding over my back, meandering. I'd missed this. There's the buzz i drive my arm into his right tit my fist resting sixteen inches below his skin ripples the crackle of signals through it whirring speeding boundless.

We come open to the main sauna. Cyborgs and androids fucking in every shape, bonded and loving, ecstasy beyond anything flesh-bound. My chaperone kisses the back of my neck and whispers:

'G o o d luck.'

The first time I fucked Victor was the moment I fell in love with him. Everything changed. Everything collided with itself: the warmth of his soul, his eyes, his cock. Part of it is every tiny chaotic short-circuit at the peak of coexistence, tiny apocalypses bursting all over the place. That's what real beauty is. Beauty needs other people. Beauty is the flail of the orc in the throes of orgasm, throwing himself against taut restraints, being seen in all one's depths and chasms. This is where I need to be.

I wander through the floor. I stabilise. I notice protein counts, metallic bonding, alloy consistency and properties of knee bolts, skimming over a controlled, logical flood of straight flat stale information; it grounds me. I take everything in, making sure I know where I am. The exit is 11.2 metres away, 11.8, 12.2. This is where I want to feel safe, so I need to make sure of it. I catch the gazes of occasional people; most are going at each other, but some are looking round. Big, powerful doms waiting to be served, bound in leather, ambiguous skin or clothing, eyes like diamonds: glistening, hard, gorgeous. Others don't have eyes. Others just wait with a few hungry submissives crawling round, hunting for the right feel of contradictory safety. Two hulking orcs argue with a smaller cogspirit. I disregard it; it has nothing to do with me.

I decompress my neck valves, the signal to those of a certain type, and keep an eye on the door, not leaving that 15-metre radius. An enhanced older orc crosses the room, marbled skin and grey-eyed with gently glistening tattoos. I feel his soft metal brushing my back, it's there, something magical, gentle as anything, whispering destruction and pain and horror and love. His memories wander gently into my mind: a factory accident, the years-long gelling of cheap metal into tough skin, the adaptation to electronic perception, the death of his husband, the grieving, healing. In return, Victor drifts across. This is another man in search of safety here. He speaks, with the kind of voice that makes you want to retreat into someone's arms.

'H e l l o there b e a u t y'

I turn to look at him, muscles relaxed, primed, waiting for someone, metal tendons a spiderweb over his chest, covering one arm, his neck, chin, and most of his lower half. I reach out and run my fingers over the tendrils, twirling the stiff, tightly curled chest hair, then drift down between his legs. He smiles, and bends down, and I am washed, cleaned, wet tongue against cold metal.

We move to a booth for something like privacy, but still public, still there, still scenery for wandering eyes. The tenderness found in a fist, beyond a fist, beyond physical bodies and space and moving into the literal sparks between us, friction and static and beyond, behind, between any definitions of being one mind or two. His grief surges through my body. My circuits, my glistening exhaust, are wrenched aside in hunger, leaving just mind and feeling. His skin and bioflesh wet and soft, the smooth shine of his extensions, toying with my body and far beyond it. His husband and Victor embrace, gazing from a place of memory, a beautiful concrete illusion but feeling, becoming, more powerful, immaterial. No time nothing null, no perception no life. Everything dissolving under a healing wave of pleasure and violence, flushing out every thought, tearing open every mental wound, left as vulnerable as could be, living through each other's pain, cycling through memories and claw marks, skin torn from chest and back, metal bodies bent and buckled and gouged open. The terrible violence of his cunt destroys me, pierces me, undefines me my grief my soul my death. The world vanishes, everyone vanishes, the gap between dead and the living vanishes, thoughts cease while all there is to know is hurt and pleasure, felt together, existing as oneness, a wholeness beyond anything, no connections. We are the only thing, and we are the entire universe, no definition no perspective. The exposed wires and leaking insulation fluid where the plates hung, gored and half-torn from my back, are Victor's funeral pyre, our private mausoleum.

∫

Leaving my nameless saviour with a kiss and a silent word of thanks, I wander across the hall to the repair suite, aching with new grief for this other dead husband. Our slime-cyborg host exposes his opal teeth to me, reading my changed battered aura and my open wounds as sites of peace. Over the warm bed, the dim violet lights blink in the reflecting surface of my gnarled skin. I drift through the systems in the room, the strangely-wired exploratory recovery booths, the same homeostatic firmware as in my house, an inkling of the everyday in this not-normal place. Fingers of heal-enhanced Aloe explore my tears, my burns, my scars. I am put back together, the pink sludge of nanomachines knitting wounds together stronger. I stay there till morning, dreaming of Victor, and this life beyond him. This is a step. This could help. I could carry on, maybe. Here I am.

∫

The sun rises as I walk back along the canal. The last remnants of the healing sludge evaporate, so I steam as I walk, steadily losing my pink aegis.

∫

It's been 239 days since my husband died

SYNCHRONICITY

RIEN GRAY

Kell had always known they were expendable.

Only certain types of people ended up on a scrap ship, after all – washouts from tech programmes and the military, or the last wet gasps of outer-world cloning facilities. Kell was the latter. Upon maturation, they were given a genetic scan and pronounced devastatingly average, save for some hormonal imbalances that added another mark on the 'unsuitable' column. After being booted off the homeworld, there weren't many other places to go.

Scrapping was dangerous work. Most vessels and debris floating in dead atmosphere were picked clean by the oldest, most industrious crews, and whatever they left behind was a lethal gamble. A golden warship adrift in space tempted everyone, but most were spewing radiation, an invisible death knell to whoever landed onboard looking to scavenge. Everything else was garbage, collected only to be stripped down to raw materials and sold in bulk for a fraction of their worth.

But a sealed trade ship hanging out near a wormhole?

That was something in between, especially when it was boarded up for a biological hazard.

'That's what that symbol means, right?' Haoyu said, tapping the scanner. It was older than he and Kell put together; to call the device inconsistent was perhaps too generous. 'They evac-ed, then locked up. Didn't report it to the authorities, either.'

'It's a blockade runner,' Kell replied, tracing the shape of the vessel with a fingertip. Long, lean, and fast enough to slip past border control. Governments were deeply paranoid about alien contamination on their precious planets, but rich folks loved the exotic, and would kill each other for one-of-a-kind finds. 'Whatever's in there, telling the authorities would have gotten them shot into space.'

'So which one of you scabs is going in there to find the prize?' Captain Inessa boomed from behind.

Kell tensed. The captain was one of the few exceptions to the scrap ship rule: as a pilot she had survived a decades-long career pacifying asteroid-side rebels, but peacetime made her redundant, especially when new politicians wanted to paper over last term's genocide. Inessa looked down on all of them, and she did it with a smile. Her 'scabs' nickname started to stick a few months ago, after one of the first-timers miscalculated his trajectory and plastered himself across an opposing ship. There had been nothing to do but peel him off and recycle the waste.

'Grab one of the new guys,' Haoyu answered, too quick to hide his nerves. 'Whoever pops that seal is probably dead.'

'Probably,' Inessa admitted. 'But I need someone experienced on the inside. I don't trust the recruits carrying anything worth more than my left tit.'

The fake one, of course. Kell swallowed a laugh, but Haoyu was starting to sweat. Inessa's eyes were locked on him, and the captain never liked to make a decision twice. If she told Haoyu to grab the haul, his odds of survival went down twice over: either risk going in the ship, or get executed for insubordination.

His boyfriend lived on one of the border worlds, some cute guy from Neo Hong Kong working on a solar farm. Kell knew how long Haoyu had been saving to escape the scrapper life, skipping meals to earn his one way ticket out. They, on the other hand, hadn't had so much as a hookup in months.

'I'll do it,' Kell said, loud enough so Inessa couldn't pretend she hadn't heard. 'Strap me up, boss.'

Haoyu's eyes snapped wide. 'Kell, you don't have to – '

'Rather call it quits now instead of doing twenty more years of this shit,' they interrupted. 'At least this way, I might strike it rich.'

'True.' Inessa smiled, serpentine. 'Carrier gets twenty percent.'

Guilt pulled Haoyu's face down like a mask of lead, but he managed a small nod of gratitude. 'I'll get you ready.'

There wasn't much to do. Kell stripped and worked the short-term exposure suit up to their hips before leaving the rest to Haoyu. The protective material had started out high-vis white and incredibly tight, sealing the wearer in against the worst that space had to offer. Now it was the colour of old bone and needed a little extra suction to do the deed. They would have to open the suit back up after reaching the other ship, before it became impossible to sweat and breathe.

'Looking good,' Haoyu said, fitting the helmet and its miniature oxygen canister in place. 'Feng isn't here, so I can say your ass is incredible.'

Kell laughed, fogging up their mask. 'If I'm going to go out, at least I'm hot, right?'

The two of them shared a weary smile, only to flinch as Inessa's voice carried from the onboard speakers. 'New kid cracked the ship. She's alive, so go get my money, Kell.'

Maybe that was a good omen. They sure hoped so.

It was only a twenty-foot drift from dock to dock, but with a single cable holding them to the rest of the universe, Kell saw the void like an ancient country mile. Sans gravity, they landed on the emergency exit in complete silence, and wrenched its huge red lever open. They slipped through the open door and into a pitch-black decompression chamber. The hatch hissed shut, plunging them into darkness.

Once the pressure stabilised, Kell felt around for the next latch. As on most models, it was low and to the right, but their hand slipped off twice before catching. Something impossibly slick covered the metal, and they prayed that the substance was just mechanical runoff from a cold life-support battery working overtime. The well-lubricated latch keened when Kell twisted it.

Emergency lighting shocked their eyes as the chamber opened, running along the floor in bands of blue. The ship's walls were cast in strange shadows from spools of gut-like cable hanging from the ceiling, ripped out with brutal force. Kell had never seen anything like it, or the silver sheen dripping from the cables, swollen and eye-catching as mercury.

'Probably as dangerous as mercury too,' they muttered, and carefully stepped past the pools of liquid by their feet.

The further they went, the more destruction they found. One deck of the ship had been completely scoured by fire, leaving behind ashen skeletons of furniture. Past that, a hallway was riddled with laser fire, and a handful of actual bullets. Kell was tempted to dig into the wall for remnants – whoever funded this ship had to have been obscenely rich – but couldn't shake the sense of how wrong everything was. No one risked open flame on a sealed vessel, and firing weapons onboard could kill everybody by proxy.

Everywhere, the silver fluid held dominion. Entire rooms had fallen under its scintillating influence, but Kell couldn't figure out the source. It slipped through every crack and gap in the ship like water, but thickened and set like chrome after swallowing something whole. If this was Inessa's prize, they had no damn idea how to package it for delivery.

Or if doing that was safe in the first place. Kell reached for their mask and took a deep breath, hoping that it wouldn't be their last. The seal popped, and air spilled across their sweat-drenched face, cold but clean. They reached for the collar of their suit next, tugging until it opened to bare their chest.

'Okay,' Kell whispered. 'Not dead.'

They grabbed an empty cup from one of the only untouched tables and held it under a nearby vent, dripping with promise. A heavy drop of fluid splashed into the cup, spreading out across the bottom. Kell tilted it to look closer, only to panic when the liquid twitched and swelled, lunging at them in the blink of an eye.

Silver struck their mouth and held it still, open, before pushing between Kell's teeth in a single solid thrust. Bitter heat coated their tongue in a shining skin. They choked, trying to force it back out, but a colloidal clot slid down their throat and disappeared. Kell waited for pain, for nausea, but there was only more warmth, spreading low through their belly and up through their skull. Then a voice filled their head, stretching from ear to ear like a malevolent thread.

Be mine? Static hissed and popped between every syllable. Mine.

Kell flinched. 'What the hell?'

Be mine, it repeated.

The fluid in the room surged around Kell in massive waves, held at full crest and eager to fall. Even with fear punching holes in their chest, the sight was beautiful, shining like captured starlight. Every muscle in Kell's thighs clenched, stomach pulled taut and low as desire lit up their nerves. Another electric jolt went right between their thighs, leaving them both rock hard and dripping wet, friction rubbing against the tight cup of the exposure suit.

'Is this you?' Kell asked aloud, breathless. 'Is all of this you?'

Yes. The voice was inside them, but it flowed through the waves too, pulsing like a heartbeat. Be mine.

Another tender shock followed; Kell bit back a groan. They throbbed, hips yearning to jerk forward. The suit was suffocating, and it was so tempting to rip it off and spread themself wide. When was the last time they felt so good? Never, maybe. Pleasure was for people who could afford it.

'Are you going to hurt me?'

No. The static faded. Now it hummed, soothing. Mate.

Kell would have laughed at how absurd this was, if not for the fact that being fucked by a so-called biological hazard was preferable to being killed by one. 'Yeah, all right. Do it.'

Every wave crashed at once, covering their entire body with metallic fluid. A sound like acid startled Kell until they realised their suit was the only thing being devoured, the barrier replaced with thick, ever-shifting tendrils. They couldn't see or move, but when one of the tendrils thrust deep inside, bliss blotted out the rest of the world anyway.

Both of their nipples hardened, trapped by a vacuum-sealed suction, pressed against a taut silver skin. Kell tried to catch their breath, but a solid, glistening mask had full custody of their face, and another cool protrusion pushed into their mouth, sinking to the back of their throat, thick and unyielding. They shuddered as the fluid sought their third hole, tighter than the rest, but despite the lack of slickness, there was no pain. It molded to their insides, a deep and perfect shape.

Even with pleasure singing through their nerves, Kell felt panic bubbling up in their lungs, taking over for the lack of air. They couldn't talk, couldn't signal, but the silver subtly parted around their nose, allowing two tiny pathways to freedom. The sudden burst of oxygen made them clench tight around the exploring fluid, so quick and ecstatic that Kell saw sparks like constellations, devoured instantly by hungry black holes.

More, it whispered, then hummed again.

This time the vibration spread through Kell's entire body, inside and out. They weren't sure if the sensation was more like being massaged or fucked, but the combination overwhelmed everything but the primal urge to be touched. They longed to touch, to somehow participate, but enveloped in the seductive silver, Kell could only suck and lick at the smooth shaft filling their mouth. Yet that had some effect; a deep bass sound echoed inside their skull, lingering like a whale's song, needy as a groan.

Kell's first orgasm swept them into an undertow of ecstasy, too powerful to deny, every shining current pulling them in deeper. They whimpered and choked, offering up animal sounds in place of a name they didn't know. The vibration spiked in intensity as the fluid swelled, opening Kell wide, pushing so far that they briefly imagined the silver as a single thread impaling their entire body. Surely it couldn't, or if it could, they wouldn't survive –

Another soul-shaking release shattered their thoughts entirely. Kell's body went slack, trembling from the white-hot bursts between their thighs, but they couldn't fall, not while surrounded by something so strong. They wheezed for breath, having so little to spare, and the vibration slowly tapered away.

Good mate, the voice slipped up the back of Kell's neck like a lover's tender touch, you feel good.

You too, Kell wanted to say, but what came out was a choked gurgle.

Then the fluid shifted again, pouring away from their face and melding with the mass around Kell's shoulders. Even that much freedom felt sublime, leaving them panting for a good minute before finding words again.

'What are you?' they asked.

Stolen. Anger rippled through the fluid, contorting its shape. Seeking a mate, when the ship came.

They guessed said ship tried to shove the silver into a container, and the second it broke loose, so did all hell. That certainly explained the bullets and fire, although from what Kell could tell, the fluid was entirely immune.

'Do you have a name?'

Its answer was a vast and incomprehensible burst of static, rubbing along the inside of Kell's skull. They coughed, shivered, and mumbled apologetically, 'Okay. I'll work on translating that. Mine's Kell.'

Home is so far, the fluid whispered. Where is yours, Kell-mate?

'Uh, I don't really have one. Citizenship's hard to come by these days,' Kell said.

Let me stay. We can search together.

'I...' They looked down at the morass of silver that was

keeping them glued to the deck. 'Not saying no, but I can't move like this. In case you didn't realise.'

A curious thrum followed, and Kell gasped as the silver transformed entirely, smoothing out along their body from head to toe. If they didn't know better, it could have been mistaken as one of the exposure suits, form-fitting but flexible.

Better?

They clenched a fist as a test; there was no resistance or complaint. 'Way better.'

We can live like this, the voice added. It sounded, of all things, vulnerable. I will provide.

Kell raised a brow. 'Provide how?'

Oxygen. Sustenance. Pleasure. In open space, we can feed at will.

An organism like this would be worth millions, maybe even billions, to the right buyer. Kell knew they just had to make it to a planet with one of those galactic media feeds, and the fluid would sell itself. Yet –

They could be free. Free to travel the stars without a single credit in hand, without losing themself to new wealth. Buying citizenship would be easy, but it meant a life locked up in a clean atmosphere, ignoring everyone exploited outside the bubble. Anyone who tried to help the less fortunate got booted right back out.

Hooking up with a hot alien symbiote sounded like a dream in comparison.

'All right,' they answered aloud. 'Let's blow this wreck and look for where you're from.'

I sense another ship near this one. Will they not search for you?

'Don't you worry about that,' Kell said with a smile. 'I'm expendable.'

PERSONAL TIME

JEM NASH

The package arrived the day before he did. I'd been pulling a lot of all-nighters at the lab so it was only when I opened it and saw the strap-on that I realised something was up. I'd clearly spent too long thinking about string theory and ordered it in a fugue state. I must have. Because it was perfect. Exactly what I had envisaged. And I hadn't even been brave enough to Google it.

He showed up not long after I got home. I was exhausted from work and, for a moment, I thought maybe I was hallucinating when I pulled the door open and came face to face with myself.

'Hey, Gabe,' he said. 'How's things?'

Not wanting to be rude, I let myself in. He nodded as he passed through the hallway, pausing to toe off his shoes. It was only while he was looking around the place that it hit me.

'Oh shit,' I said. 'It worked.'

'Not yet,' he said, turning away from inspecting my bookcase to look at me. 'But soon. Give or take a few years.'

'You solved the Grandfather Paradox? Or has this all happened before for you?'

'Come on, we're smarter than that. It's multiverse theory, baby.'

He had been searching around and made an 'a-ha' face before pouncing on the mystery box.

'You sent that?'

'Yup, cost me an afternoon but it'll be worth it. Trust me.'

'It came yesterday.'

He cocked his head to one side. 'I'm not touching that one. But, yeah, sorry, I thought it would get here today,' he smirked. 'You must have been going mad wondering who sent it.'

'I thought maybe it was me and I didn't remember.' I huffed out a laugh. 'I suppose that's kind of true.'

Other Gabe hummed to himself. 'Best not to think about it too much. Side effects may include headaches and permanent damage to the space-time continuum.'

I pushed unfinished equations out of my head to ask: 'Do you want a drink?'

'Sure.'

'Yeah, I figured. If I'm still so horny in the future that I invent time travel to get laid, I definitely need one.'

I tried to get it out of him but Gabe was playing our cards close to his chest.

'You don't want to know anything.' Theoretically I knew that was true but I couldn't stop myself from asking.

'You're on testosterone,' I noted as I passed him a beer.

'Yep,' he said, looking at me drily before taking a sip.

I sighed. 'If you're not going to tell me anything, why did

you come back?' Gabe put his head on one side in a way that I didn't consider a habit yet. 'Ok, we weren't kidding. This really is a one-track trip.'

'Well,' he said with a smile. 'I was hoping maybe more than once.'

And oh shit, yeah, I was kind of hoping that too.

'I don't really know what the etiquette is for this situation.'

'You think I do?'

I flopped onto the sofa and looked up at him. 'I'm assuming you've travelled before.'

'Not like this.'

'You've never visited other versions of me? Of us?'

'I've never travelled for this purpose before.'

'Ok, well then why now? Or, then?' I waved a hand. 'Whatever.'

'I had to save up my frequent flyer points.' He finished his beer and discarded the bottle on the nearest shelf. 'I really wasn't expecting you to fixate on the logistics of this so much.'

'You're sure you're not from a radically different timeline? Because the fact you didn't feel compelled to put that–' I nodded towards the bottle he'd drained – 'straight in the recycling makes me wonder if we're even the same person.'

'We chill out a lot in the future.'

'Huh.' I fiddled with the label on my own bottle. 'What's your favourite movie?'

'Gabe.'

'I just – I figure we're a bit different in other dimensions. I kinda want to know how different.'

'We're the same enough that I came back to have potentially paradox-inducing sex with you. How different can we be?'

'Forgive me if I need a little sweet-talking before I put out.'

Gabe sighed and came over to sit next to me on the sofa. He leant back against the armrest. 'My favourite film is *Starship Troopers*. 'Do you want to know more?"

I laughed and put my half-finished beer aside. 'Nah dude, we're good.'

I leaned over and kissed him. It's strange to think of it as making the first move when it's with yourself. But good for me all the same. I'll say now that the kissing was the weirdest part. The rest was kind of just advanced masturbation but having your own tongue in your mouth twice is wild. It took a while for us to adjust to not giving each other what we wanted at the same time. It's hard for you both to suck on the other's lip simultaneously.

Once we'd figured out a rhythm I pushed him back and straddled him. A jolt ran through me. Sure, it's a little perverse to be turned on by yourself but, sexually, everything is relative. I ground a leg between his and, from the sound he made, the hormones were doing their job.

'Buy a guy dinner first,' he quipped breathlessly.

'Hey,' I murmured, as I snuck a hand up his shirt. 'You were the one who didn't want to talk.'

Gabe hummed his assent against my mouth and I ran a thumb over his left nipple. He breathed in sharply. I sat up.

'Aha! You felt that!'

'Yes, of course I – oh.'

'Yeah, currently rightie does most of the heavy lifting.' I brushed back over it and Gabe swallowed and made a strangled noise. 'I guess this means the nerves grow back eventually.'

We looked at each other. Gabe wasn't giving anything away but if this was an alternate timeline there was no guarantee that was the case. I tried to ignore that thought, and the myriad implications that came with it, and started undoing the buttons on his shirt.

'So, what are we going to do?'

He grinned. 'Everything.'

Despite the strangeness, we made out for a while. I mostly kept my eyes closed but my hands mapped out this newer version of me. Our bodies were different enough that there was something to explore. Gabe had broader shoulders, fun to grip and feel the muscles moving beneath as he ran his hands through my hair. Tingles crept over my scalp and I breathed in deeply through my nose. He even smelt different. Still the same citrus shampoo scent but beneath that a warmer, lustier aroma. He had more body hair than me and when he ran his palms up under my sleeves every follicle of mine stood on end. I could feel myself getting warm and irresponsible. He was wearing jeans so I had the added benefit of denim-induced friction as I ground into him. Gabe made a filthy noise that went straight to my crotch, along with half the blood in my body. Kissing became increasingly difficult as we both got more and more worked up. I was making noises lower in my throat than I thought possible and Gabe was pushing his hips up to meet my own. Then we both tried to go in for each other's neck at the same time and almost cracked our skulls together. I laughed, breathily.

'Your left or my left?'

Gabe snorted and slid his hands up my T-shirt. I tensed.

'Still all good?' he asked.

I swallowed and nodded. 'Yeah.'

He gave me a knowing look before pulling my shirt over my head. 'We'll go slow.'

Slow, for the record, felt pretty fucking fast. When you're riddled with anxieties about sex even hooking up with yourself is intimidating. But the whole point of this was to get over that so I put my big boy pants on (or rather, took them off) and got down to the job at hand (coincidentally, a hand-job). Even relocating to the bed was a little nerve-wracking at first. Then Gabe was on top. He pinned me down gently but firmly and I could feel my body expanding with my lungs beneath his soft grip. He let the memory of his hands hold me down and sat up to slowly undo my fly. His eyes never left mine. Somehow, with a grace I had not yet mastered, he manoeuvred himself so that he could skin my trousers off me. I did however recognise his decision to leave my boxers on. I'd learnt by now to stop asking and I decided to chalk this up to kindness rather than continued discomfort. Or maybe we just had a kink.

Gabe took my wrist and said: 'Show me.'

'But you know,' I replied.

'Yes, but you need to learn how to tell other people.'

So I took a deep breath and slid his hand under my waistband. I placed his index and middle finger either side of my dick so that it felt more like, well, a dick. He buried his left hand in my hair and tugged slightly, then murmured into my ear, 'Relax.'

His right hand started moving in a way that was almost shockingly familiar, drawing me up in one solid motion and letting me grow in response to the sensation. It was just like every time I'd jerked off for the past three years. It was nothing like anything I knew.

Gabe licked my right nipple and I felt it rise to meet him, just like the rest of me. I moaned and tried not to think about the pitch of my voice. His hand kept moving and when I arched into it he sped up. 'Oh god.' I gripped the sheets with one hand and his arm with the other. Oh god oh god. Then I had one of those orgasms that feels like consecutive waves of pleasure and makes you shake like your brain just abandoned motor function. Which, considering how much we were messing with the laws of conservation, maybe it had.

Gabe rolled off to one side. 'I know what you're thinking,' he said cryptically. 'I know you wish it was just one orgasm and done like' – he made quotation marks in the air – "normal guys'. But trust me, you're going to miss multiples. It's not a bug, it's a feature.'

I still felt slightly debauched but that cut right through my pupil-blown stupor. Not that I had any idea how to respond. Gabe didn't seem to mind though and was already getting up. 'We need to hydrate. Then it's round two.'

After chugging my glass of municipal cocktail, I let Gabe strap me up and I mentally strapped in. He'd had the forethought (hindsight?) to bring condoms because, as he well knew, I wasn't having sex with anyone so didn't have any lying around. I wasn't even doing elaborate forms of self-gratification. Gabe knelt in front of me to roll the condom on and lube us up. And, hell, was that hot.

'Ok, we're going to ease into this–'

'That's what she said.'

He stood up and gave me a dry look to contrast how wet we were both getting. 'Right, I'll get ready and then if you stand–'

'Will you show me?' Gabe seemed almost taken aback. That was kind of its own thrill – I could still surprise myself. 'So I know for... in the future.'

He clambered onto the bed and guided my hand down to circle his arse with my slicked-up fingers. Time slowed down. Gabe eased my fingers in and made a low sound in the back of his throat. One day my voice would sound like that. After a little more preparation he swallowed and said, 'Ok.'

Together we guided my added length slowly and gently into him. This involved a lot of breathing on his part and a lot of freaking out on my own. And then he said, 'You can move now.'

I was hesitant at first. I didn't want to hurt him and I wasn't really sure what angles would work. But I solve unsolvable problems for a living and Gabe wasn't exactly quiet so whenever something sounded good I stuck with it. Eventually I got a steady rhythm going. The base of the strap-on was pressing against my own hard-on. Thrusting felt euphoric.

'F-faster,' Gabe gasped. So I did as I was told and soon we were both groaning in octave harmonies and he was occasionally choking out an 'oh fuck' between ragged breaths. I refused to call out my own name during sex so I took a leaf out of my own book and swore as I came. My hips kept on moving of their own volition but for once I was alright with them doing their own thing. Then I heard Gabe finish and all but fell on top of him.

Somehow I instinctively knew it was almost time for Gabe to go back (to the future). But he spent a few more minutes with me, both of us lying with the sheets pooled around our waist. I laid a hand over his scars, more faded than my own.

'I kind of miss them,' he said, reaching out to trace mine. 'They meant so much to me.'

'I know what you mean.' I smiled slightly. 'Everything else is... but them I like.'

Gabe's gaze softened and he withdrew his hand. 'I know you don't want other people to like your body because you don't. But you gotta get over that. Because people will want you the way you are and that's a good thing not a hardship, you muppet.'

I managed a very quiet thank you. For a minute I thought he was going to kiss me again but instead he reached out and ruffled my hair. 'This meant a lot to me too, in its own weird way.'

PERSONAL TIME

I dressed while he showered. I felt like I'd just had the best, strangest therapy session of my life. As I showed him out, Gabe stopped in the hallway and hugged me, like he was trying to answer all of the questions he'd evaded with that one gesture.

'Look after yourself.'

And then he was gone.

I was planning on going back to bed when I had a timely thought. So instead I went to my desk and started to work on our future.

HER HANDS MOVED SHIMMERING ACROSS ME

ANNA WALSH

Sadie (formerly Sad Lady to her students) moved her hands across the tablecloth in her new kitchen. Her door was open, and from the hallway she could hear sparks crackling from the open fusebox. She briefly considered the dangers of damp housing and raw electricity. This new flat was better than her aunt's house, even if it was old, older than her family tree and probably older than St. Anne's School for Girls too. The Gorbals was made up of construction sites and closed shops, and old Georgian buildings housing young families and solitary older people, like herself. According to the letting agent, she was lucky to have even secured the drafty flat. Vegetation and glittering rubbish stalked up out of the rocky concrete from Glasgow city to her new home: to the untrained eye they sometimes appeared as single homogenous growths, small blue blossoms of Haribo plastic entwined in the wild garlic and brambles.

She left small gifts for the other people in the building. She folded stiff cards with her schooled handwriting inside, and placed them outside each door beside four homemade buns. She had made the buns in her old house and carried them to the new one in clear tupperware. She had not counted on the attic being occupied, and, after giving away all the buns, left a hastily-bought cactus on the landing beneath the ladder instead. She wanted to write PLEASE DON'T SQUASH ME! on the note, but instead wrote, *to the occupier of this attic flat, from your new neighbour at 3-1* and left it at that. None of the occupants ever knocked on her door. She was grateful for it during the first week, but became suspicious when she never saw another person in the building, not once. She spent her days going up and down the three flights, organising and redecorating her small flat, and in her spare time she walked around the area, smiling at those she passed by.

Several weeks passed, and although she was on chatting terms with a family across the road she had still not met anyone who lived in her building. She heard noises most nights, from both the attic and the flat below, but she couldn't intuit what was happening. She assumed, as she had done when she was on retreats with the teenagers she taught, that whatever sounded sinister in the middle of the night was more than likely harmless. She was a heavy sleeper anyway; thumps and the odd wail didn't bother her.

On a damp, grey Tuesday evening, after a depressing phone call with her sister, Sadie decided she would go for a late walk. November blurred the streets and sky into a hard, consumptive grey and Sadie picked at her neat leather gloves while completing her usual circuit: twice around the small, foggy square, up and down the main street, and back again with a small bag of chips. She was far more relaxed about treats now that she was finished with the school and her family, and she felt more or less comfortable and happy in the new building. Her sister was angry, as ever, because she now had the responsibility of their elderly aunt, but Sadie didn't care much. She had felt over the last few years that she was entering a new stage in her life – one she would have welcomed thirty years prior, but that was still equally as enjoyable at present. She only wanted for company and felt certain that it would eventually turn up, like it always did. Someone, somewhere, would be willing to sit and talk with her; she would just have to wait. In the meantime she was organising her finances, taking stock of her books and papers, even joining up to beginners' classes at the local Govanhill swimming baths.

As Sadie took the stairs up to her flat quickly (privately impressed by her new fitness levels), she was irritated by the scent of ginger and something else difficult to identify. She stood for a moment and took a deep sniff. The scent was richer, hazier now, and coming from the door on the second floor. It made her lick her lips. Taken by a sudden courage she knocked on the door of the perfumed apartment. A short, thin-faced woman answered.

'Hello!'

The woman looked up at her, her eyes brown and wide. 'Are you alright?'

'Me? Yes! I just wanted to say hello.'

'Oh? Hello?'

'I live upstairs.'

The woman stepped back and gestured into the hallway.

'Want to come in?'

'Now?'

'Yeah.'

'Oh, thank you! I wasn't, didn't mean to intrude–'

'Take your shoes off there, thanks.'

'–yes, that's no problem, thank you for inviting me in!'

Sadie smiled brightly around the hallway as the woman retreated to a dark, cloudy room and returned with a small cup. She followed the woman into a different room, a small sitting room full of large, colourful cushions that looked like plump sugar cookies, the floor covered in luxurious rugs. The woman pointed to the pink and green couch, which Sadie understood to be an order. She sat into the soft, velvety fabric and wiggled her stockinged toes out in front of her. The woman sat with her legs wide apart and relit the small brown joint.

'Is this alright?'

'Oh yes, of course. I'm sorry, I didn't mean–'

She waved her hand at Sadie, shaking her head.

'Don't worry about it. I've been meaning to call to you. You're upstairs?'

'Yes, three-one. It's a very nice building, I have to say.'

'Have you met anyone else?'

Sadie laughed.

'Not quite. I expect people are more private than myself. Or at least that's how it seems to be.'

'Well, I'm not. My name is Ann McKeon, I'm forty next year, and I run a medium service from my home. From this room, actually.'

'Oh! Well, my name is Sadie Wilson, I'm a retired school teacher and I believe I am to turn sixty in a year or two.'

Ann nodded, and held the joint towards Sadie. Sadie reached over, her small legs tingling from the static of her stockings against the couch, and took a light pull.

'Do you not think I'm mad?' Ann asked.

Sadie exhaled, the fumes silky and fragrant between them. 'For this?'

'Don't be polite. I've just told you I run a medium service.'

Sadie always felt the bliss come from her feet first and smiled as it rose warmly up to her belly, her lungs, fizzing in her throat and ears. She shook her head.

'This seems to be a nice way to live. Have you been doing it for a long time?'

'Twenty years. I used to do it in a circus and then in town. It's much easier from here.'

'Do you have many clients?'

'Enough to keep me going.'

Sadie nodded, liking the conversation. She lifted one of the plump pillows and put it across her knees, gently slapping it. Ann laughed.

'Enjoying that?'

Sadie smoothed the pillow and held it to her chest.

'Do you ever take on new clients?'

Ann stubbed the joint and moved the ashtray to the coffee table.

'Sometimes. Is there someone you want to speak to?'

'Not particularly. But I am very intrigued.'

'Fair enough. I can do that for you. But not today. I'm wrecked today. Come back tomorrow.'

Later, as Sadie floated up the dark stairs back to her flat, she thought she felt someone watching her from the landing, glowing white in the cool, blotted darkness.

When Sadie returned the next day, she brought homemade carrot and ginger soup. She told Ann she had been compelled to make it when she got into her kitchen, the gingery fire of the soup prolonging her high.

'You are a funny one. Thank you though, and you can just sit where we were yesterday.'

Sadie sat back in the same spot, perceiving a stillness in the room that she had not felt yesterday. Ann came back wearing a loose white shirt and trousers, holding several candles. Something about the way she dedicated herself to her tasks made Sadie feel affectionate towards her, like they were longtime friends and she could count on this trait of Ann's. She moved her chair to face Sadie before lighting a candle in each corner of the room. When she sat, she took Sadie's hand and spoke in an even, professional tone.

'I cannot ensure that you will have any contact with those who you seek tonight. I am a vessel, most often a physical one, one that cannot control or call specific spirits to me. I can relay their messages to you. I will voluntarily enter the trance state, and you will meet those who enter me. You must not worry or fear for me. I am a willing vessel.'

Sadie felt old and silly, and stifled a laugh. She nodded solemnly as she looked into Ann's tired eyes. She liked how soft and warm her hands were around her own.

'I will now enter the trance state. I will return once the session is over.'

Ann closed her eyes and hummed quietly. The noisy reverb made Sadie feel tickly, and she wished Ann would stop. She hummed no tune but rather a monotonous flat sound and, as quickly as she started, she stopped. Her legs were wide apart, almost enveloping Sadie's own, and she suddenly lolled back into the seat, pulling Sadie with her. Sadie fell on her knees onto the worn carpet and she felt the scrape of friction move up her bare legs underneath her long skirt. Ann did not release her hands; she grasped them closer to her body until Sadie's head was squashed comfortably against her torso. Her pulse beat in Sadie's ear. Ann began to speak in what sounded like a tinny, emptier version of her own voice.

'Are you a ghost too?'

Sadie paused, feeling the muscles of Ann's stomach contract. Her lips made contact with the linen of Ann's shirt as she responded.

'Yes. I think so... I feel like one.'

'Yes.'

'Nobody sees me.'

Ann's arms gripped Sadie around her waist, hoisting her back to the couch. She walked towards the corner of the room and picked up a candle, the flame burning almost white in the room. She handed the candle to Sadie.

'Do you feel beloved?'

The question made Sadie want to cry. Ann's glazed face was disturbing to watch as it spoke, almost as though being manipulated by a lazy puppet master, pulling the strings too slowly. Whoever was in Ann right now sucked on Ann's teeth and moved slowly back to the chair. Notes of contented pleasure came from her and she did not blink as she looked at Sadie. There was nothing behind the brown eyes and her mouth had curved up into a mocking, unnatural grin.

'I want you to feel beloved. I want you to know several things: I am an object possessed, I will possess you, and everyone yields to me.'

Desire cut through Sadie's groin. She felt oily and melting in the small room as Ann stared through her. She wanted fiercely to go to the bathroom and touch herself, felt it in her teeth that she wanted Ann without clothes, wanted to see what she looked like bare and open. The strength of her desire frightened her. Ann began to pluck at the buttons of her shirt, lifting the white linen from her body. She did not wear a bra, and sat back in the chair, the mute shadows flickering across her arms and shoulders, small moles dotted across her clavicle. The candle was hot in Sadie's hand and she felt like she was standing in sand watching the tide rush out beneath her. She knew she wanted Ann to place something hard and dense inside of her, wanted something pushed into her mouth, her throat. She was overcome by a feeling she had only felt once or twice before, when she was a young teenager. She felt beautiful to herself and she enjoyed the legs she now rubbed together under her skirt, the painful tingling in her nipples and lips. She moved as though hypnotised, turning to face the wall and raise her skirt, dropping her old-fashioned, dusky pink underwear. She heard Ann mumble something, and she blew out the candle and handed it back to its owner. Her new muscles kept her upright as she stickily spread her legs, and Ann put her warm hands on Sadie's ass, pressing a finger to where she was wet.

'I see you. I always see you.'

Sadie heard Ann spit and felt the cool slickness of the candle against her anus. Ann rubbed the object between Sadie's legs, dragging it across her inner thighs and along her lips. Sadie had not been touched in so long that she felt like she was dying, and she pushed her hips violently back into Ann, silently begging her to put something somewhere hard and fast and immediately. Ann dropped to her knees and licked Sadie with her warm tongue, from behind her knees all the way up to her asshole, and once again spat on the candle. She placed a hand on Sadie's back, and with the other, began to massage her with round circles of her thumb before pressing firmly in, pushing inside. Sadie's body seized up and she panted, pulling and twisting at her breasts, her cheek now pressed hard against the wall.

'Please!'

Ann grunted behind her. Sadie felt the foreign object penetrate all the way into her anus, Ann's fingers stroking her clitoris and the candle thudding into her in a slow, alternating rhythm. Sadie grabbed behind herself at Ann's legs, jerking back and fucking herself faster, moaning now and feeling split open, feeling opened out like a wet, greasy pastry, crying out to be fucked harder, harder, more things inside of her now, a candle in her mouth, another in her cunt, Ann lying across her back sweating and working, Sadie with tears in her eyes swallowing hard objects, penetrated from every angle feeling possessed, feeling wild, feeling full of a white glowing light, like she had been finally recognised, no, exposed for what she really was, and the humiliation made her insides crack and split as she glistened, riding Ann, saying she didn't care, and once she came they both fell onto the couch covered in ooze and sweat, talking and crying to someone who was no longer in the room with them but continued to watch from a distance.

BOY IN MAID OUTFIT FOUND DEAD HANDCUFFED TO RADIATOR IN GIRLBOSS' BASEMENT 11/08/2024

ALISON RUMFITT

There was a boy dressed in a maid outfit found dead handcuffed to a radiator in the basement of a female CEO's Hampstead townhouse last week. Second one this year. Different girlboss both times. Some say there's an epidemic. Once is a tragedy, twice is a serious problem. A sort of societal rot. Of girlbosses. Of boys in maid outfits. Of handcuffs. Of Hampstead. That sort of thing. You ever looked around Hampstead, looked at all the houses there neatly lined up like some sort of Richard Curtis film? Walked from the Waterstones where some bitch signs her books in real life through a residential street curling towards the Heath, then across the Heath up in the direction of Highgate maybe, towards the Ladies' Pond, where you want to go for a swim? It's a pleasant walk. I go all the way up to the Ladies' Pond sometimes and stop, just short of the fence, and that is where I turn back around to retrace my steps all the way back to the tube station again. Maybe I stop at a café on the route back, if I can afford it, sometimes even if I can't. Like today. I stop anyway, and have an overpriced frappuccino with whipped cream on top. I look at them all, at the posh people in the sun outside walking their dogs, and the posh people in here, on their laptops, reading, on their own. I look at my phone. I scroll through Tinder. There are dating apps designed specifically for the rich, designed within an inch of their lives, by their very nature exclusionary: you have to know someone who knows someone, sign a secret contract with ink made from truffle-pig blood, attend some sort of masked *Eyes Wide Shut* kind of deal and suck off a Hollywood actor just to get your foot in the door. Just to get the mere opportunity to swipe left or right on your betters and have your betters swipe left or right upon you. I don't have access to those apps, of course, I could never get through the front gates, so I have to stick to one of the more mainstream ones. I rarely ever get matches, but that's fine. Looking at people is more fun sometimes than speaking to them.

It's about three in the afternoon, and a strikingly attractive woman enters the café, face shaded by big sunglasses and a floppy black hat. She has a face I might recognise, but it's so obscured by the shadow from the hat and the sunglasses that it's impossible to get a grasp on who it might be; and even then so many rich people look like other rich people because they can all afford the same best-in-the-business surgeon. Hot woman orders a matcha latte, stands there at the counter bouncing up and down on her heels impatiently, looks down at her phone like it's made of maggots and then snatches the drink when it's handed to her. She leaves as fast as she arrived. If I wait here long enough I wonder if another exactly like her will enter and order the same drink, and leave with the same fury.

Not that I think all women are the same or whatever. It's just here; all the girlbosses, swarming around the wine bars and the coffee shops. So many of them. The one who had just been here, had she been one of the female CEOs who had fallen prey to an S&M accident? The police report said neither death was connected, said neither death was being treated as suspicious. It could have been that one for all I know. Were the radiators on? Did the handcuffs, metal, surely, heat up and burn the boys' wrists with deep red rings? The ice in my drink has melted, it's turned into a sludge. There's a buzz, and a notification from an app saying I have a match. I open the app, but the match doesn't show – guess they just unmatched immediately, probably an accidental swipe right. Probably. It takes until I get back to my place for me to look at the app again and see her, right there at the top with a circle next to her name and a message sent right to me. I could have sworn it was her, the woman from the café. Her message simply says hello. Becoming very aware of the presence of my heart beating inside of me, I message her back, hi there, and the moment the message has been sent I put the phone face down on the other side of the bed and try to avert my eyes from it and look at something else. I look at my laptop screen or the shit 24-inch TV, but the moment I do that I hear it, I hear the buzz, and because I can't see my phone screen I don't actually know if the buzz means she already replied or if it was just a marketing email or a spam text and I'm too scared to check at least for the next minute and a half. I wait, eyes going from laptop to TV to window to the blank back of the phone and then looping again until I can't take it anymore. I grab the phone, feverishly, and see that yes, she replied. She asked me how I am. She asked me how I am and how long have I been here and where did I live and what did I think about Brexit and what did I think about the Tate and who I am and why was I here and it's like she is stuck on the roof of my room, looking down at me, shining like the morning star. She asked me how I was and what I was up to. I look at the pictures on her profile; none of them are her in the hat or the shades so I can't be sure. Every time she messages I think about how rude she was to the barista.

I ask her to tell me about herself. She owns a bespoke neutral-tone baby clothing business. She doesn't have kids, but she was inspired to start the business when her sister had a daughter and complained that all the rompers and so on were bright pink or bright blue, too overly gendered, and I say I understand because at least I think I do.

I still don't know why she's talking to me though. It's the thing that brings me down throughout the day as our conversation tumbles and turns. After every message I wonder if I should ask her what she wants from me, some overweight twenty-one-year old in a single bedroom flat that smells slightly stale. She flirts with me, tells me she likes the way I look, sends a picture of herself at the beach the previous summer. I masturbate to it, starting with my dick and then, as I get closer and closer to orgasm, shoving the two middle fingers of my right hand inside my asshole to stroke my prostate until I want to fucking scream, eyes connected with hers in the image, eyes connected with her cleavage in the swimsuit in the picture on the beach last summer wish you were here. I feel gross afterwards and don't shower.

That evening she says it again, got to go to bed now, got loads to do tomorrow morning, but will message in the afternoon. I don't doubt it. I saw a tweet about how you shouldn't wank to someone without their permission. Everyone was making fun of it online for about two days straight. It's obviously wrong, she was flirting with me anyway, that's why she sent me that picture. So why do I feel so fucked up?

She walks into the café at exactly the same time as she did before – hat, lipstick, shades and all – and I start to wonder if this is a good idea. She has been messaging me from about one o'clock onwards, telling me about how shit her morning was, how the place she sources her fabrics from was fucking her over on prices and how she needs to find somewhere better. She looks up and doesn't recognise me at first. Not until she does. Her face goes from hostile to warm.

'Oh!' she says. 'What are you doing here?'

I don't blame her if she's suspicious. I would be suspicious, too.

'I come here sometimes!' I say.

'But it's so far from you!'

'Yeah but... the coffee tastes so much nicer here for some reason. Everything tastes so much nicer here.'

'Wow, look at you,' she says, appraising me, appraising my fucking fat thighs and my double chin but still smiling. She looks so good. The pantsuit she's wearing must have cost a thousand pounds. It hugs her figure. 'Gosh, if I didn't know better,' she smiles, 'I'd say this was a little creepy.'

I blush. 'I promise, I guess we matched because I come here often, like I promise it's nothing weird,' I start to babble before she cuts me off with a giggle and tells me everything's okay.

'You know,' she says, 'I'm nearly done for the day, and some of the girls are coming over for drinks at six if you'd like to join us. I'm sure they wouldn't mind.'

'Wait, really?'

'Of course.' She smiles like a snake in a children's film would smile. Her in the swimsuit, her on the phone to some investor. 'Come with me, I don't live far from here.'

'You look like the morning star,' I mumble as she grabs my hand and pulls me out of the café, but she doesn't hear.

She lives in a townhouse, with plants at the front, with windows as big as my bedroom door in every room, with furniture I couldn't sell my organs for everywhere I look. There are piles of clothes everywhere, crumbs underfoot. Guess she's so busy with the baby clothes that she doesn't have time to clean.

'What's down there?' I ask, pointing at the one door she hasn't shown me.

'That's just the wine cellar,' she shrugs. 'The girls will be here pretty soon,' she says. 'You should get ready.'

I follow her to her bedroom, and there, laid out on her bed, is a maid dress.

'This place is a fucking state,' she whispers in my ear.

'Oh?'

'Look at it. Get it cleaned up now before they come. Put on that fucking dress.'

Which I do. I undress in front of her. I don't know what time of day it is, or what the address of this house is. The dress doesn't fit me, it's too small. I feel like I've been poured into it and the seams are being stretched by my awkward shape. I don't feel sexy at all. In the mirror, the person looking back at me looks like a lost little boy on Halloween, forced to dress up as a girl by his friend's vindictive sister. Blushing. But I have to do what she says. Why do I have to do what she says? I live in a place with no walls or windows or doors, a wet system of being, a blushing little boy bending over for her, picking up everything off her floors, dusting out the cobwebs from her sunny stairwell until they look like they were only just built yesterday, fat fuck with the shameful cheap anime cosplay look, the sort who people laugh at when they see him at the convention, and she watches me the whole time, her stock prices going up, erect like my dick, the maid dress getting even tighter. The girls are coming soon, the other girls.

'They're all business owners,' she says, 'the girls. We get together for drinks sometimes. It helps us focus.'

When they enter, they are all nearly identical to her, dressed in sheer trousers and blazers and hair up above their shoulders, sharp red lipstick. They walk in and don't acknowledge me at all. Standing there, red in the face, dick clearly visible to all of them. They don't even seem to see me. Why not? I just cleaned this fucking flat for you bitches, and you won't even look at me, you won't even see me, it's like I was never born, a poor little nobody crawling out her mother's cunt beneath the eaves of a house in the middle of nowhere, strewn with needles and human shit. But I can't speak. Even if I want to. Mistress has taken my tongue and locked it in a box which she wears around her neck. I can see it, hanging on a chain, hanging between her two ample breasts.

'Shares are down again,' says one of the girlbosses, not taking off her shades even indoors. 'Already. It's been so soon since the last one.'

'Do you ever worry that the more we do it, the less effective it becomes?'

She shrugs. 'It works as a business solution for the moment. Shares go down, then they go up again after. If it stops working, we'll stop doing it, but for as long as it works, if it means doing it every single day, I'll do it.'

I'm on my hands and my knees, they have put a silver plate of canapes on my back and are eating off of it. When the plate is empty, she makes me stand up.

'We need some wine,' she says, first time addressing me since the girlbosses arrived. 'From the cellar.'

I mouth yes, mistress, but don't say it, although I feel the tongue inside the box around her neck twitch like a phantom limb. I go to the door, and look back one more time over my shoulder at the women all sitting around on their chairs, legs dutifully crossed, each of them with a box around their necks. I open the door and head down into the dark cellar. The wine lines the walls in racks, and in the middle of the room candles burn together in a circle, the only light at all down here. My hand is under my skirt the moment I get down there, in the cold basement. My hands are cold too, it almost hurts as I start to jack off. She's at the top of the stairs, looking down at me. They all are. Watching scornfully. I start to whimper like a little puppy the closer I get to orgasm, and just as I'm about to come, just as my other hand is fingering at my asshole, all of the candles in the centre of the room go out, and I feel them all around me, and here and now for the first time ever I can feel how much I'm really worth.

So Mayer is a queer feminist writer, bookseller, organiser and anarchival cyborg. Their most recent textual pleasure is *A Nazi Word for a Nazi Thing* (Peninsula, 2020).

Adam Zmith is author of *Deep Sniff: A History of Poppers and Queer Futures* (Repeater Books, 2021), co-producer of *The Log Books* podcast, and a dirty little space cadet.

Gracie Beswick is a Glasgow-based writer originally from Leeds. Since the library she worked at closed down she has had to start writing her own stories instead, and she now works as a Museum Assistant by day and a writer by night. As a former Sex Education teacher she loves writing that discusses sex in a positive and inclusive style, particularly when it involves aliens. Although fairly new to fiction her non-fiction writing on literature and lifestyle has been featured in *Flip Screen* and *Qmunicate*. You can find her thoughts on books, writing and the vital importance of saving public libraries at @graciebeeswax.

Rachel Dawson is from Swansea, and she currently lives in Cardiff with her wife. All her writing is inspired by the resilience of our queer ancestors, and the joy of loving other women. In 2020 she was one of the twenty-five writers awarded a bursary by Literature Wales.

Diriye Osman is a British-Somali author, visual artist, critic, and essayist based in London. He's the author of the Polari Prize-winning collection of stories, *Fairytales For Lost Children* (Team Angelica Press) and his work has appeared in *The Guardian, Granta, The Financial Times, The Huffington Post, Vice, Poetry Review, Prospect, Time Out, Attitude* and *Afropunk*. His second collection of stories, *The Butterfly Jungle*, will be released in summer 2022 by Team Angelica Press. Diriye lives on a diet of Disney cartoons, ersatz elevator jazz, graphic novels, masala chai and Missy Elliott records.

Swithun Cooper's work has recently appeared in *Magma* and *A Queer Anthology of Healing* (Pilot Press). His poetry has won an Eric Gregory Award, and in 2019 he was an Emerging Writer in Residence at the London Library. He is currently working on a novel, *The Long Fight*, inspired by his real-life experiences with undercover police and queer activist communities.

Nicks Walker is a queer bigender trans ex-Catholic, lapsed Scot, horse mistruster and vapourwave nuisance. He writes all sorts of things. You can find his objects in *SPAM, Rejection Letters, Punk Noir Magazine* and elsewhere on The Internet, as well as in some (but not all) books, including *The Speculative Book 2021* and A *Drunken Midsommar*. His allies include yellow, and his enemies include the sun. Find him in the bird dimension @nickserobus.

Vivien Holmes is a writer, musician, and organiser based in Manchester. She has been published in *Salt Magazine, Fruit Magazine*, and *Black Telephone*, is a staff writer at *Country Queer Magazine*, and works with Partisan Collective and Trans Mutual Aid Manchester. She plays guitar in Ether Mech. She doesn't like olives.

Rien Gray is a queer, nonbinary writer with a focus on F/F and F/NB romance and erotica. They have an ongoing romantic suspense series featuring a nonbinary assassin starting with *Love Kills Twice*, as well as an F/F paranormal romance out in October called *Her Wolf in the Wild*. Rien enjoys writing kink, hot monsters, and morally ambiguous queer protagonists. When away from the desk, they're usually either at the gym or trying way too hard to 100% a video game. You can find them on Twitter @riengray.

Jem Nash is a trans writer based in London. When he isn't creating his own queer stories he can usually be found reading other people's and has a particular passion for science fiction. Fueled largely by tea, he works part-time as a bookseller and is currently studying for his MA in Gender, Media and Culture.

Anna Walsh is an Irish writer living in Glasgow. Their poetry has been published by the *Stinging Fly, Bad Betty Press, SPAM* and others. They write fiction and essays, some of which appear in the anthologies *So Hormonal* (Monstrous Regiment Publishing) and *Outsiders* (3 of Cups Press), elsewhere in

Abridged, Gutter Magazine and *Extra Teeth*. They are writing a novella and a short story collection. In their spare time, they co-run the Trans Writers Union.

Alison Rumfitt spawns in marshland from September-October every year. Her debut novel, *Tell Me I'm Worthless*, was published by Cipher Press in October 2021. Find her on Twitter @hangsawoman.